THE SOMEWHAT TRUE
ADVENTURES OF
SAMMY SHINE

Published by
PEACHTREE PUBLISHERS
1700 Chattahoochee Avenue
Atlanta, Georgia 30318-2112
www.peachtree-online.com

Book and jacket design by Nicola Simmonds Carmack
Composition by Melanie McMahon Ives

The illustrations were rendered in pencil

Printed in July 2018 in the United States of America by LSC Communications in Harrisonburg, Virginia
10 9 8 7 6 5 4 3 2 (hardcover)
10 9 8 7 6 5 4 3 2 (trade paperback)
ISBN 978-1-56145-866-0 (hardcover)
ISBN 978-1-56145-778-6 (paperback)

Library of Congress Cataloging-in-Publication Data

Names: Cole, Henry, 1955– author.
Title: The somewhat true adventures of Sammy Shine / by Henry Cole.
Description: Atlanta, GA : Peachtree Publishers, [2016] | Summary: When his
  toy airplane crashes, a pet mouse becomes lost in the woods.
Identifiers: LCCN 2015025798
Subjects: | CYAC: Mice—Fiction. | Airplanes—Fiction. | Toys—Fiction. |
  Forest animals—Fiction.
Classification: LCC PZ7.C67345 So 2016 | DDC [Fic]—dc23
LC record available at *http://lccn.loc.gov/2015025798*

THE SOMEWHAT TRUE ADVENTURES OF
SAMMY SHINE

HENRY COLE

PEACHTREE
ATLANTA

For Kathy

Contents

GOGGLES' WORKSHOP

GOGGLES' OLD TREE

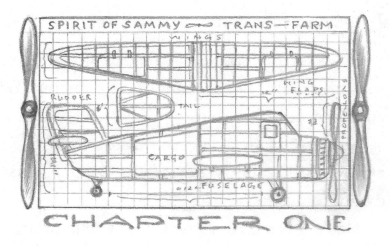

SPIRIT OF SAMMY ∞ TRANS—FARM

CHAPTER ONE

The door to Hank's room flew open. "It's ready!" a voice called out.

Hank looked up from his drawing. "What's ready?" he asked.

His brother stood in the doorway. "The plane, you ding-dong. It's ready to fly." Jimmy glanced around the room. "Where is he?"

Hank put down his pencils. "It can't be ready," he said. "The paint isn't dry yet."

"The paint's dry, the motor is all set to go, I got fuel, it's ready." Jimmy's eyes landed on a shoe box with holes punched in the lid. "He in there?"

Hank sat up straight. "Yeah, but...are you sure it's safe? I mean, it's not going to crash or anything, is it?"

"It's practically uncrashable." Jimmy sounded annoyed. "Perfectly designed. Totally aerodynamic."

Hank gulped. He trusted Jimmy. His brother could design and build anything, turning wood and wires into something amazing. But this time the stakes were high.

Hank remembered when his brother had first unrolled the large sheet of paper with the words "Spirit of Sammy—Trans-Farm" boldly lettered across the top of the page. The detailed blueprints showed a beautifully proportioned airplane delicately balanced on three rubber tires and powered by a gas engine. A tiny door opened to a cockpit at the front, just behind the engine. There was a cargo bay toward the rear of the plane.

That was only three weeks ago. Evidently the project had gone from plans on paper to a finished airplane.

"Get Sammy," Jimmy commanded. "I want to test him for weight."

"Uh...I don't know." Hank glanced at the box. "Sammy doesn't like heights. He might get airsick."

"Not in this baby," Jimmy replied. "The *Spirit of Sammy* is going to ride the wind like a pro. Steady as she goes, no pitching, no yawing, no rolling, no airsickness."

"How do you steer it?"

"Ding-dong—don't you know anything? This plane is the latest. It's RC: remote controlled. It'll fly like a dream, with me controlling it from the ground. C'mon. I'll show you. Bring Sammy."

Hank reluctantly picked up Sammy's shoe box and followed Jimmy downstairs to the cellar. Jimmy's workroom was a small, dark nook tucked behind the furnace. It was crammed with all manner of tools and parts and pieces, remains of past projects, and beginnings of new ones: drills and saws and soldering guns, jars of nuts and bolts and nails and bits, rope and tape and glue and paints, pliers and screwdrivers, dead batteries, scraps of wood, dismantled flashlights, stubs of pencils, and old telephone dials and broken speakers and radio insides, everything scattered and piled in all directions.

Sitting proudly in the middle of it all, glistening with and smelling of fresh dark green paint, was the *Spirit of Sammy*. She was perched on three tiny rubber  tires, and seemed almost impatient to take to the air. Her name was emblazoned across the fuselage in Chinese red letters.

Hank stared in awe.

"See this?" Jimmy picked up what had been an old square cookie tin. It was wrapped in electrical tape and adorned with dials, switches, and a long antenna. "Found most of the parts I needed at the junkyard." He twisted one of the dials. "This controls the wing flaps. And this one controls the tail so I can turn it."

Jimmy picked up the small plane and pointed inside. "See the little wires inside the cockpit? It's just like in a real plane, connected to the rudders and everything. There's even a throttle. Sammy could fly it himself if he had a brain. I even made him a flight helmet. But the

remote control does everything. Amazing, if I do say so myself."

"So what do you need Sammy for?" Hank asked.

"What's the point of flying a plane if there's no passenger?"

Hank squinted at the device. He wasn't convinced. "Well, what about if the plane crashes?" he asked. "Is it safe?"

"Totally safe."

"Will Sammy have a parachute?"

"A parachute? Oh, jeez." Jimmy rolled his eyes. "Look, he won't need a thing. He can sit back and relax. It'll be like a vacation for the little squirt."

"I refuse to let Sammy die in a plane crash."

"Why are you always such a dope?" Jimmy swept a hand through his hedgerow of thick brown hair. "Here's a chance for Sammy to be something great...to go down in history."

"You're nuts."

"You have no imagination. Listen; think about when the local papers get hold of this. You, me, Sammy? We'll be heroes. Maybe even front page news!"

"Yeah, right," Hank sniffed.

"No, really! There'll be a picture, I'm sure of it. Me holding the *Spirit of Sammy*, you holding Sammy. Everybody smiling." He jerked his thumb at a newspaper clipping on the workroom wall showing Charles Lindbergh standing next to his airplane. "We might even get *Popular Science* or *National Geographic* interested."

"I don't know...."

"Everybody at school would hear about it. If you had any friends they'd be begging for your autograph."

Hank pondered for a moment. *"National Geographic?"*

"Sure!"

"I dunno...."

Jimmy ignored him. "The day has got to be perfect. I mean really perfect. Either no breeze, or a breeze from the south. Clear, no rain. The latest weather report says that tomorrow's supposed to be just right." He looked again at Hank. "Have Sammy ready and prepped tomorrow at eleven hundred hours."

Hank gulped. "You guarantee that Sammy will go up and come back? I mean...alive?"

"He goes up a rodent, comes back a hero. He'll be the mouse version of Lucky Lindy."

Hank lightly tapped the side of the shoe box as he lifted the lid. "Hey, Sammy," he whispered. "You ready for high adventure? You

18

want to take a trip across the county? In an airplane?" He saw a pink nose and a pair of soft gray-brown ears poke out of a bed of sawdust. Dark, guileless eyes peered up at him.

It was too much.

"Sammy stays on the ground," Hank said firmly. "Go get another pilot. A grasshopper or something."

"Huh?"

"You heard me. Sammy is out."

Jimmy's face reddened. "That's the thanks I get. I build an airplane that could make you and your stupid mouse famous. But no! You have to go and be a chicken!"

"I'm not a chicken! I just don't want Sammy to die in one of your crazy inventions."

Jimmy turned and stomped up the cellar stairs. "That plane is totally safe," he shouted over his shoulder. "And don't worry. The *Spirit of Sammy* will have a pilot. You can bet on that!"

CHAPTER TWO

The morning sun was just slanting in low from the east when Hank lifted the shoe box lid to check on Sammy. He saw the familiar lump in the sawdust, so he closed the lid again and hurried downstairs for his breakfast. The windows were open, and sweet summer air permeated the kitchen. It was going to be a perfect day.

He was just about to lift a forkful of pancakes to his mouth when he heard a noise.

THWOP...THWOP...THWOP!

It was coming from the lane, next to the

barn. He knew that sound. It was Jimmy trying to start the *Spirit*'s engine.

Hank slammed down his fork and raced up the stairs, taking them two at a time.

He burst into his room and yanked off the shoe box lid. The lump in the sawdust was still there.

"Sammy?" Hank asked. "Sammy?" He gently touched the lump.

It didn't move.

Hank poked the lump again, then brushed away some of the sawdust. The lump was just a wadded up piece of paper.

"Jimmy!" Hank howled. "You rat! You're really gonna get it!"

He half ran, half slid down the stairs, streaked out the screen door, and headed to the lane.

Just then the gas engine started up. Its high-pitched whine filled the air.

Hank ran as fast as he could past the barn and up to the lane that pointed north to the woods.

Jimmy was crouched over the dark green *Spirit of Sammy.* "Stand back!" he warned, his voice barely audible over the screaming engine noise. "The propeller blades!"

Hank skidded to a halt. "You are such a jerk!" he yelled. "Give me Sammy!"

"He's fine!" Jimmy shouted. "This is it! Takeoff!"

With a triumphant yell, he lifted the *Spirit of Sammy* high. But as he launched the plane into the air, he stepped backward. His left foot landed squarely on the remote control, snapping the antenna and crushing one of the dials.

The *Spirit* took off in a streak of dark green.

Jimmy snatched the metal box off the

ground; the antenna and some wires dangled uselessly.

Hank stared at it in disbelief, horrified and speechless.

The plane had already risen from ground level to fifty feet. It caught a slight tailwind and headed northward.

"Golly," Jimmy whispered.

"Sammy!" Hank cried.

Jimmy snapped to. "It's really moving! Let's go!"

They raced across the field, eyes on the sky, trying to keep up with the plane. They scrambled over a barbed wire fence, tracking the *Spirit of Sammy* by the buzzing whine of its engine, which got fainter and fainter.

"Oh, jeez…." Jimmy scanned the sky. "Where is it?"

"There!" Hank pointed north. "Holy cow!"

The plane was now barely visible, just a dark dot in the blue sky. They could no longer hear the whining engine.

A moment later, it was out of sight. It was too high and too far away for them to see.

"Wow," Jimmy said quietly.

Hank scanned the sky again and again. "Sammy is gone," he said, choking back tears.

The *Spirit of Sammy* was in the air.

Sammy was at the controls.

"Help!" Sammy squeaked.

The plane careened to the left and he was pitched into the cockpit door. Then it tilted to the right and he slammed into the other side.

The *Spirit of Sammy* wobbled this way and that, and Sammy tumbled about the cabin.

"Oh, brother!" he cried out, as if there was any chance of someone hearing.

The plane lurched and pitched beneath his feet.

He saw a thin metal bar in front of him

and he grabbed for it, holding on fast. The bar moved under his weight, pulling to the left, and the plane zoomed to one side. As he pulled the other way to steady himself, the plane zoomed in the opposite direction.

Pulling on the metal bar made the plane respond! He gripped it with determination.

When the plane swayed to one side again, Sammy tugged the bar the opposite way. The plane steadied itself.

He glanced outside; he could see little flapping parts moving up and down on the wings.

"Aha!" he shouted above the engine roar.

He caressed the bar, moving it this way, then that way, and the plane obediently followed his directions.

He was steering!

He felt like doing a little jig. He banked the *Spirit of Sammy* almost on one side, then carefully

reversed the move and banked the other way.

He saw a lever that stuck out from the floor, and, feeling a bit more confident, gave it a short pull. The *Spirit of Sammy* dipped forward and began plunging toward the ground.

"*Aieee!*" Sammy screamed. "Oh please, oh please, oh please!" He pushed the lever the other way and the plane pointed upward and then leveled off.

Sammy realized he'd been holding his breath. "Whew!" he sighed. "Up, down, left, right…lots to consider!"

A thick copse of trees loomed ahead. It was directly in his path.

"Oh, please, oh please, oh please!" he murmured under his breath. "Up…UP…*UP!*"

He pulled on the lever hard but steadily and the plane reacted immediately, zipping delicately just above the treetops. The window

filled with a view of blue sky and puffs of white clouds.

Giddy with exhilaration, Sammy played with the controls, doing a bit of a barrel roll and then a loop-the-loop.

Then he noticed something: there was a small gauge directly in front of him. There were big red letters on it: *F* and *E*. A green arrow was just to the right of the middle, between the two letters.

"What the heck could that mean?" Sammy said to himself.

He studied the little green arrow. It jiggled, but he could tell that it was very slowly heading toward the *E*.

"Something tells me that I'm in trouble," Sammy groaned.

He had been flying for what seemed like forever. The scream of the engine was nearly deafening, and his ears were ringing. His tiny body shook from the vibrating plane.

He pictured his cozy, quiet home back in Hank's room, and longed for the peace and tranquility of his shoe box. It was time to turn around.

With steady paws, he gripped the control bar tightly, and slowly maneuvered the plane into a long, arching U-turn to the east.

Through the cockpit window, he could see fields and forests below him, a patchwork of green.

The morning sun swept across the windshield, temporarily blinding him. He squinted and blinked, but didn't see the top of a tree as the wheels of the plane clipped it. The plane suddenly dipped into the woods, too hard and too quickly for Sammy to recover.

In seconds the plane was smashing through clumps of leaves and sideswiping branches. Sammy was thrown to the floor of the cockpit, then to the ceiling, then side to side over and over again. His head banged sharply against the metal bar and he squealed out in pain.

The *Spirit of Sammy* was going down.

He pulled and yanked at the controls,

narrowly missing an enormous tree trunk, then another. He swerved and banked, steering between tree limbs the best he could. Oak and poplar leaves beat against the windshield. It became impossible to see out.

"AAAAH!" he screamed, throwing up his paws protectively.

A second later the plane crashed into the underbrush of the forest floor with a hard jolt.

The dizzying onslaught of oak leaves turned to blackness as Sammy's head hit the windshield.

CHAPTER 4

Sammy struggled to sit up, still woozy and shaky. He was dazed and bruised and dizzy, but alive.

The *Spirit of Sammy* hung on its side and dangled a few inches above the ground, caught in the weeds and spicebush branches.

Soft light poured into the cockpit. The door was jammed by the branches of a weed. Sammy pushed against it, and it opened a bit.

He poked his head out through the narrow space, and then squeezed his whole body through and plopped to the ground.

He blinked, alert and wary. His nostrils filled with smells he didn't recognize, nothing like the sawdust and peanuts he was used to. It was fresh and clean and fragrant. The sweet scents of millions of flowers and the earthy smell of rich loam wafted over him. The very air was unfamiliar, but wonderful.

A forest of lilies towered over him with glossy emerald leaves leading like stepladders up to bright orange and lemon yellow blossoms. Viridian fern fronds wove in between the lilies, and pastel purple columbines grew among the ferns. Red and black butterflies hovered over brilliant white and yellow oxeye daises, violet wood sorrel, and lavender wild petunias.

Sammy stood still, amazed at the rainbow surrounding him.

Beyond the tall lilies were many giant trees. Enormous oaks, elms, poplars, and beeches stretched to the clouds, their topmost branches rustling and swaying in the breeze.

Something buzzed behind him, and he pivoted in a flash. A green creature hovered nearby, and Sammy froze. It gave him a casual glance and then buzzed away.

A shrill call came from one of the trees. Something else mysterious, this time with striking black and white and red feathers, climbed along the trunk of a tree, pecking and exploring the knotty bark.

He heard a vibrating hum from behind, and he spun about, terrified. Another creature, smaller and quicker than the others, hovered just an inch in front of his face. Its wings beat so fast that Sammy couldn't even see them.

The dazzling, iridescent feathers shocked him; he had had no idea that something so incredible existed.

Before Sammy could say hello, it was gone.

Another sound, this time from something vermilion and chocolate brown, traveling with amazing speed across the ground. Its hundred legs undulated in perfect synchronized rhythm.

Sammy stared as it quickly scuttled away.

He heard a twig snap, and he wheeled around, expecting to see another astonishing woodland marvel.

Instead, he found himself facing a semicircle of field mice. Each of them carried a spear

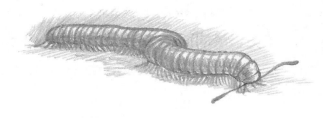

made from a stick, with a long, glistening por-
cupine quill lashed tightly to the end, sharp
and barbed.

The hairs along Sammy's spine tingled.
"Uh…hello!" he stammered nervously. "Hello?"

CHAPTER FIVE

The armed mice stepped back and raised their spears.

Sammy didn't want to be lanced, but he wasn't sure what to do next. "I...come in peace?" he ventured.

One of the mice stepped forward, and Sammy gulped. The mouse crouched, head bowed, and laid his spear on the ground in front of him. "Hail!" he squeaked loudly.

The other mice crouched as one, spears flat on the ground. "All hail!" they shouted in unison.

"Huh?" Sammy mumbled. "All what?"

The first mouse seemed to be the one in charge. "At your service," he said.

Sammy looked around. Apparently the head guard was speaking to him.

"Uh...thank you," Sammy said. "Thank you very much. I...I...uh. Well, where am I?"

The head mouse looked surprised. "You are in the Great Woods."

"'The Great Woods'? Where is that?"

"It's...here." The head mouse seemed puzzled. "The Great Woods is here. It is the name of this forest. Who are you?"

"My name is Sammy...Sammy Shine."

The head mouse nodded at the airplane suspended in the weeds. "Yes, Sammy Sammy Shine," he said. "Your method of travel—it clearly says you are a spirit, and I would guess a very powerful one. We would like to know if you come with good intentions."

Sammy looked up at the plane. It dawned on him that the woodland mice saw him as some kind of alien from another world.

"Oh! Well, I would say definitely my intentions are good ones."

"Have you been sent here by Mustela?"

"Who's that?"

The mice looked at one another.

"Mustela," the head guard repeated.

"I don't know any Mustela."

"That is very good news, oh Spir—uh, Sammy Sammy Shine," said the guard.

"What...what's it like to fly?" one of the younger mice asked. "To go anywhere you want?"

Sammy wasn't sure what to say. He was still dumbfounded by his journey through the air, and slightly dazed from his crash landing. "Flying is...amazing," he replied. "You see the world as a leaf on top of the tallest tree would see it. You see the sky from edge to edge. You see how big things are. And how tiny you are."

The other mice gazed at Sammy, wide-eyed. "Wow," the young mouse murmured. He pulled at his whiskers in excitement.

"Perhaps you are hungry after your journey," the head guard said. "We would be honored to take you to our Lodge. It isn't far."

Sammy wondered what a lodge was. But he was hungry. "Sure," he answered. "That'd be great. Lead the way!"

Then he stopped, gazing up at the dangling *Spirit of Sammy*. His heart did a little flip. The landing gear was broken, a branch poked through the fuselage, and at least one wing flap was ruined.

It was his only way home. He thought about
Hank and his old shoe box. It already seemed a
long time ago, another world.

It looked like he might be in the Great
Woods permanently.

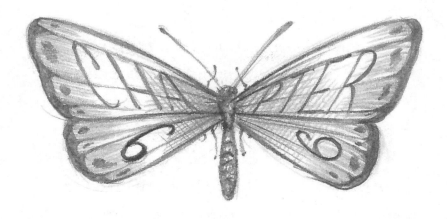

The *Spirit of Sammy* had landed near a small trickling stream, which explained the lush, almost magical vegetation and variety of flowers that grew there.

The group set off into the woods. Massive trees towered over them. Their branches arched and entwined together high above. Sunlight streamed down between the leafy layers of the forest canopy, creating green-gold patterns everywhere.

They climbed up a hill, along a narrow path through a thick tangle of ferns, and under and over enormous tree roots. The trail was clear and clean and well maintained. Calls and songs echoed from all sides: trills and warbles and chips and caws.

The mice crossed the creek, using a mossy tree trunk as a bridge. They traversed giant boulders and passed through a tunnel made from a fallen log.

Finally they reached their destination. A large flat rock jutted out of the sylvan hillside, half covered in vines and wildflowers. Beneath the rock was a hollowed-out area, with a floor of hard-packed dirt.

Sammy sniffed the air; it was cool and earthy.

There were dozens and dozens of denizens on all sides in the cavernous space under the boulder and lined across its top.

Apparently the whole community had turned out for Sammy's arrival.

All of their eyes were on Sammy.

A deer mouse sat on a bench in the middle of this tableau. He was a little hunched, and the fur around his nose was gray, as were his whiskers and the tips of his ears. He leaned on a carved walking stick and stared intently at Sammy.

Beside him sat another, smaller mouse with black whiskers, white paws, and a small, pink nose. Her mouth curved up at both corners in a sort of half smile, and her pink tail was draped delicately across the bench. Her fur was tawny, like an autumn oak leaf. Her eyes were the color of late-summer honey. She seemed to be watching everything—and everyone—with calm intelligence, but also kindness. Sammy liked her immediately.

The head guard bowed to the elderly mouse. "If I may, Old One, I would like to present Sammy Sammy Shine."

"Ah!" the aged mouse squeaked with pleasure. He struggled to stand, using his walking stick as support, then gave up and sat back down with a sigh. "The one who came from Up! He fell through the trees! Is this the one?"

"Yes, Old One," the guard replied. "The very same."

"Amazing. We are so delighted to have you with us, Sammy Sammy Shine. Welcome to our Lodge. It is a very unusual day when a surprise guest arrives literally out of the blue! Welcome!"

"Thank you, sir," Sammy replied. "I appreciate the hospitality."

"I am Osmund. Or the Old One, they sometimes call me. This is my great-great-great-granddaughter, Phoebe. I try to make things simple and just call her my granddaughter."

Sammy nodded politely to the young mouse. She nodded back, looking directly at him.

"It is an honor to have you with us," Osmund continued. "We are hoping you will share at least some of your magic with us during your stay in the Woods."

Sammy gave a nervous smile. "Magic?"

"Yes! You fly through the trees and clouds like a bird, but you have the appearance of a mouse! If that isn't magic, I don't know what is!"

Sammy cleared his throat and stroked his whiskers. He saw the admiring eyes all around him and felt the tips of his ears turn pink. "Oh…it's nothing, really. Well…uh, yes, I guess you might call it magic."

"Of course it is! I understand you fly on a bird with no feathers!" Osmund laughed, tamping his walking stick against the hard dirt, and turned to Phoebe. "Magic! Isn't that right, my dear?"

Phoebe looked pointedly at Sammy, smiled, and raised an eyebrow.

Sammy gulped.

"Yes, Grandfather," Phoebe said. "Perhaps Sammy Sammy Shine would take us all into the air, flying on his mechanical bird."

"Splendid idea! Although I, of course, am too feeble for that sort of adventure."

Sammy felt uncomfortable. It was only hours ago that he had been screaming in terror over the treetops, and now he was pretending to be an expert aviator. He thought about the broken plane. How would he ever fix it?

"Uh…it would be an honor," he gulped.

"Marvelous! But right now, we must feed you. I suspect you're famished. Ho, there! Bring some food for our guest, Sammy Sammy Shine!"

"Begging your pardon, Osmund, sir, but could you just call me Sammy?"

"What? Yes of course! Sammy it is! Bring some food for Sammy! Where are the maple seeds? How about some morels? Let's have a feast for this boy!"

Out came bark platters laden with all sorts of tidbits: different seeds, beech and hickory nuts, acorns, berries and other fruits, slug eggs, and beetles. Sammy was used to his sunflower seeds and peanuts, so it all seemed very foreign.

Everyone joined in the feast, asking Sammy questions, offering him different dishes, and begging him to try this, taste that.

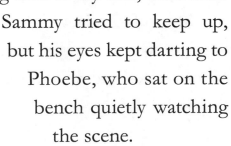

Sammy tried to keep up, but his eyes kept darting to Phoebe, who sat on the bench quietly watching the scene.

"Now, some entertainment for our guest," Osmund said. "We have quite the amusing troupe of performers. We can put on a little show for you, Sammy. And after that, maybe you would treat us to a display of some of your magic powers."

Sammy glanced at Phoebe, who hid her smile.

Uh-oh, he thought.

The Lodge became an amphitheater as the platters and remains of the feast were removed. Everyone gathered in a large semi-circle, waiting for the show to start.

Someone brought Osmund a comfortable chair fashioned from an old hummingbird's nest. The soft mosses and thistledown seemed perfect for his creaking bones.

"Let the show begin!" he announced once he was settled in, and everyone cheered.

Two large catalpa leaf curtains parted and a group of jumping mice entered the clearing,

hopping and leapfrogging in a crisscross pattern. They leaped off of each other's backs, flying high into the air, way above the heads of the crowd, their movements punctuated by high-pitched squeaks. The performance was dizzying and spellbinding, and the audience clapped and squealed in approval.

Sammy was mesmerized, but his mind kept wandering back to his promise of a display of magic. *Why had he agreed to do that?*

The jumping mice finished their routine with a flourish and then dashed to the side of the crowd to watch the next act with everyone else.

The curtains parted again, and out came something that seemed from another world; Sammy had never seen anything like it. He couldn't help staring at its waving, flaring nose, ringed by pink, fleshy tentacles. He looked at Phoebe. "Who is that?" he asked.

"That's Digger. A star-nosed mole. He's famous for his voracious appetite."

A large bark platter was carried out and set in front of the mole. It held a pile of plump, juicy earthworms, each one wriggling and writhing. The mole's tentacles started to twitch, and he pounced on the delicacies with complete abandon, biting and slurping and chewing and swallowing all in one movement.

"This guy can out-eat anybody," Phoebe explained. "Look at him go!"

Sammy sat transfixed as the mole gobbled down the whole dish of earthworms in seconds.

"A new record!" someone shouted. Everyone cheered as the mole, looking proud but bloated and a little queasy, found his way off the stage area.

Sammy stared in disbelief. "Amazing!" he gasped. Phoebe laughed.

The crowd quieted as a troupe of white-footed mice entered the clearing. They

climbed on each other, creating a pyramid. The smallest of them scampered to the top of the stack and juggled three acorns. Another tossed a large black beetle up to the young mouse, who caught it and continued juggling without a pause. The crowd cheered with enthusiasm.

Then suddenly the sounds of chatter and applause hushed, and the mice stopped juggling.

A tall weasel entered the clearing, his pointy teeth bared in a grin. His fur was dark and slick, and rippled when he moved. He wore a heavy breastplate made from an old turtle shell, but his movements were quick and fluid. His piercing eyes were like two shiny stones.

His paws gripped a leash, at the end of which was a large snapping turtle. The turtle's mouth gaped open, exposing the fleshy pink insides. Behind the weasel lurked several menacing wood rats.

"Well, well, well," snarled the weasel. "Look at this, boys. A party, just for us."

Sammy felt the fur on his back stand up, and he glanced at Osmund.

The old mouse struggled to his feet, his face filled with rage. "Mustela!" he hissed.

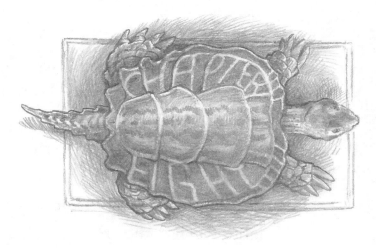

"So this is Mustela," Sammy murmured to himself. His whiskers twitched.

Phoebe gripped the edge of the bench. She glared at Mustela, inflamed but contained, like a teakettle on the verge of whistling.

"You! Out!" Osmund hit his walking stick against the bench. "You have no business here!" he fumed. "Leave this minute!"

"Not very welcoming, are you, Osmund?" the weasel replied. "I always consider your business *my* business." He chuckled and turned his dark eyes to Phoebe. "Ah...and the beautiful

Future Queen. How are you, my dear?"

Phoebe didn't speak.

"Still the defiant one, eh?" Mustela said. "Well, that's all right. You'll come around." He strolled over to Phoebe and brushed her face, stroking her whiskers. She slapped his paw away, furious.

Again Osmund struggled to stand, his ears nearly purple with anger. "You and your thugs cannot overpower us," he squeaked, his voice trembling.

"Overpower you? I'm not here for that. That's for another day. I only came for a bit of information," Mustela said. "Who entered the Woods today? A stranger." He squinted at

Sammy, studying him from head to toe. "Was it you?"

Sammy gulped. "Huh?"

"We heard a loud noise, way off in the Woods. We wondered what it was. And then a little birdie told me that you were here. And that you can fly a magic machine through the air and can take anyone anywhere."

"I...I...," Sammy stuttered.

Osmund smacked his stick against the bench. "I want you out of here!" he shouted. "Guards!"

A throng of mice, each pointing a barbed stick, surrounded Mustela and his rat cronies.

"Hmph," Mustela grunted. "I seem to be outnumbered this time." He and his pack of rats wove their

79

way past the spears and through the crowd. "You'll be hearing from me. I always get what I want." And then the gang disappeared into the tangle of undergrowth.

"How dare that scoundrel enter my domain!" Osmund sputtered. "And threaten my guest! Outrageous!"

Sammy looked at Osmund apologetically. "I'm sorry if I've caused some sort of mess," he said. "Who is he, this Mustela?"

"He is a total and complete...maggot!" Osmund sputtered. "Although now that I think of it, I have higher regard for maggots!"

"But why does he want to harm you?"

"This part of the Woods has been under my family's rule for generations. The grass is always greener, as they say. He wants this land. He wants me out so that he and his minions can take over. He's positively villainous!"

"I can see why he'd want to live here," Sammy ventured. "It's really beautiful."

"Mustela has no eye for beauty," Phoebe snapped. "He just wants the Woods for the sake of ownership, for power. And now he knows you are here, and that you came from the sky.... I'm sure he feels the Magic Bird will give him powers he never dreamed of!"

Sammy didn't know what to say. It had been an extraordinary day, beginning before dawn with a surprise wake up, lifted from his old shoe box by Jimmy's hands. Then came a terrifying flight and near-death crash. And then the discovery of a whole woodland civilization, of which he was a part, at least for a while. He'd allowed them to think he was a spirit and promised to perform magic. And now there was a terrifying, armored weasel threatening him.

What was next?

CHAPTER 9

Sammy felt overwhelmed. The day had been frightening, thrilling, exhausting. But now it was fading. Early evening light slanted through the dark, looming trees.

"How about a nice warm bed?" Osmund suggested. "The best we have, in a hidden nook. You can get a good night's sleep. The owls won't find you."

"Owls? What's *owls?*" Sammy queried.

"Owls, silly," Phoebe said. "They come out of the sky, like you did. And they swoop up behind you and grab you by the back of the head with giant claws as sharp as broken glass and carry you off, and, if you live long enough, you'll see a bird's-eye view of the forest before they eat you up."

"H-huh?" Sammy stammered.

"Phoebe!" Osmund chided. "You're scaring our young visitor."

"Don't worry, Sammy," Phoebe assured him. "We'll protect you."

Osmund held up his paw. "Come. Let me show you where your nest will be for the night."

Sammy helped the old mouse up, and with Phoebe on the other side, they slowly made their way to a crevice in between some tree roots. A small space there was stuffed with twigs, dried leaves, and bits of shredded cloth.

"Here we are." Osmund gestured. "Cozy and safe. I hope this is to your standards and that you sleep well. Tomorrow is another day, full of adventures we can only dream about. So here's to pleasant dreams, Sammy."

"Pleasant dreams, sir. Good night, Phoebe," Sammy said. "Thank you again for your kindness."

Osmund tottered away, supported by Phoebe. She glanced back at Sammy. "Good night, Magic Mouse."

Sammy crept in between the twigs and leaves and curled into a ball, tired and melancholy, and too exhausted to care about anything but sleep.

The stillness of the night was broken by a booming sound; Sammy guessed it was coming from high above his head, somewhere in the treetops.

Hoo-hoo hoohoo…hoo-hoo hooHOOO!

Sammy felt chills all the way to the tip of his pink tail. "What the…?" he whispered. "Is that what Phoebe was talking about? An owl?" His whole body quivered. He thought of home and pined for his shoe box and comfortable sawdust. He missed his peanuts, and he now saw the beetles and strange seeds and wriggling worm slices he'd been offered as repulsive.

He longed for the soft, steady breathing of Hank in his bed nearby, and the ticktock of the machine on his nightstand. His heart sank at the thought of the distance that separated him from his snug shoe box.

The rhythmic hooting grew fainter, and Sammy finally fell back to sleep.

By the time Sammy emerged from his bed, the morning sun had flooded the Woods. The entire community was up, and everyone was busy. Some were sweeping the Lodge entrance with short lengths of broom sage. Others were caring for little ones, who raced around squealing and laughing.

Most were bringing food in from the Woods. Sammy saw mice carrying armloads of nuts, bark platters full of berries, and sharp skewers of beetles and other insects.

Phoebe stood a short distance away, and Sammy scurried to greet her. "Hello! Good morning!" he called out.

"Well. How are you, Magic Mouse?" she asked. "Sleep well?"

"Yes, thank you. Something woke me up, but I went back to sleep."

"What woke you?"

"Everything is new here—new smells, new sounds. I hadn't heard anything like it before."

"Did it sound like this?" Phoebe cleared her throat, and then deepened her voice. *"Hoo-hoo hoohoo…hoo-hoo hooHOOO!"*

Sammy laughed in amazement. "That's it exactly! Maybe not as deep, but pretty close."

"You wanted to know what an owl is? Well, that was an owl. You should be glad its call was all you experienced. In fact, it's best when you hear them. It's when you *don't* hear them that you should be worried! By the time you hear the whoosh of their wings right behind you, it's too late!"

Sammy felt his whole body shiver, and he gave a little squeal. "Wow!"

Just then Sammy's stomach growled. His ears reddened with embarrassment.

Phoebe grinned. "Breakfast is served for our esteemed guest," she said.

She led him to a cleared area where several platters of food were laid out. There was a large walnut shell full of mashed crickets, a small pile of grass seeds, and some plump black raspberries. Sammy tried to ignore the crickets; his stomach wasn't ready for those. But he dove into the raspberries and nibbled one grass seed after another.

He noticed Phoebe smiling at him. "Oh. I'm sorry," he said. "Not very polite, am I? Would you like some?"

"No, thanks," Phoebe chuckled. "I had my breakfast ages ago. You slept late."

"Guess I was pretty tired."

"Yes. Must be tough being magical."

Sammy looked up at her. Her half smile was a little disconcerting. He suspected that she knew how magical he really was. "Uh...yeah. I guess it is."

"What's the toughest part, do you think?" Phoebe asked dubiously. "About being magical, I mean."

"Oh. Well, I guess it'd be..." Sammy tried to think fast, but couldn't seem to tell Phoebe anything but the truth. "I guess it'd be crashing into the ground from a great height!"

Phoebe began giggling. A moment later they were both laughing and squeaking uncontrollably, until tears rolled off their whiskers.

"I confess," Sammy said finally. "I'm as magical as you, or anybody else. It was difficult to say that in front of everybody. They all seemed so glad that I was there, and impressed by me. I...I guess it went to my head a little."

"It can be our little secret." But then Phoebe's eyes became serious. "Where *did* you come from? What *are* you doing here?"

Sammy wasn't sure what to say. "I guess I'd better begin at the beginning," he said quietly.

"That'd be a good place," agreed Phoebe.

So Sammy described his shoe box, his life with Hank, and his daily allotment of yummy foods.

"Humans?" Phoebe gasped. "You live with humans?"

"Only every day of my life," Sammy replied. "Why are you so shocked?"

"I saw a human last autumn, from a distance. I've heard lots of stories about them... scary stuff. We were all terrified."

"Scary? What could be scary? What have you heard?"

"That they're hunters. They trap us...skin us...eat us."

Sammy's eyes widened, and he choked a little on a grass seed. "Trap? Eat?"

Phoebe continued. "Everyone says they stomp through the woods. No one is safe. Fortunately they make so much noise we can hear them coming and try to hide."

Sammy was shocked. Hank had been nothing but good to him. His box was warm and comfortable. There were no owls. He had been safe—at least until Jimmy had other ideas.

"Hank was great," he said. "He made sure I

had fresh water and food. I loved those peanuts."

"What's a peanut?" Phoebe asked.

"It's so delicious. It tastes like…" Sammy smiled. "Well, I'll get you one someday."

"Deal."

"Hank never acted like he wanted to skin me or eat me. He gave me plenty of food, and he was my friend."

Phoebe looked skeptical. "Well, maybe there are good humans and bad humans. And he was a good one."

"Maybe so."

"Well, what's this Magic Bird all about?"

"It's called an airplane. Hank's brother made it, put me in it, and expected me to fly it, I guess. And I ended up crashing it into the Woods. I have *got* to get it repaired somehow."

"So you can go back? To the humans?"

"Once I've repaired the plane I'll go home. That's if I can get the engine started again. I can't imagine how I'll be able to do it."

"I'm sure you can," Phoebe said. "I'll help."

Just then Osmund tottered down the path. A young meadow mouse helped him walk.

"Here they are!" he squeaked with pleasure. "Becoming acquainted, are we? Excellent."

"Good morning, Osmund," Sammy said.

"What plans have you made for this beautiful summer day?" the elderly mouse asked.

"Sammy was just going off to take a look at his *Spirit*, Grandfather," Phoebe answered. "He wants to make repairs. Get it back in the sky."

"And you're accompanying him?"

Phoebe hesitated. "Well…I suppose."

"That would be great. Thanks, Phoebe," Sammy said.

"Be careful," Osmund continued. "Mustela knows you are here, knows of your power. Keep a sharp lookout."

"Yes, Osmund."

"Do what you can to avoid that monster!"

"Yes, Osmund."

"Stay close beneath the mayapples." The old mouse winked at Sammy. "And best of luck with the *Spirit*."

Soon they were heading down the path, with Sammy leading the way. The tall trees and masses of mayapples stretched endlessly around them. Sammy was suddenly worried he might not be able to return to the crash site.

"I hope I can remember exactly where it landed," he said. "This part looks familiar:

through the log and around those large rocks. The bridge up ahead I remember too, crossing the water. It wasn't much farther past there."

Before long they had reached the small clearing that Sammy remembered, the *Spirit*'s crash site. The tall weeds and saplings were still bent and twisted where the plane had slammed into them.

"Yes! Right here!" Sammy exclaimed. He was pleased with himself that he had been able to retrace his steps and find the spot. "And right up there is the—"

His jaw dropped.

The *Spirit* was gone.

"Where is it?" Sammy cried out. "It was right there, hanging down, caught in the branches. What happened to the *Spirit?*" He darted around and around, looking up, hoping to catch a glimpse of the green airplane in the green leaves.

"Are you sure this is the exact spot?" Phoebe asked.

"Yes! See the broken twigs and torn leaves? It was right here! Who could've taken it?"

"Look, Sammy, there." Phoebe pointed to a scraped place on the ground where some weeds had been mashed down. "It looks like maybe the airplane was dragged across here."

Sammy examined the area. "Maybe."

"And look here. See how the blades of grass are flattened in one direction? I bet the *Spirit* went thataway." She squinted into the distance. "Mustela!" she said. "He must have taken it!"

"I wouldn't be surprised," Sammy agreed. He suddenly felt marooned. The *Spirit* was his only way back to Hank, and home. Without it, he would remain in the Woods forever.

"Should we follow the trail?" Phoebe asked. "We might lose the scent if we don't."

"I...I guess we should," Sammy answered. He contemplated what to do next. *What if they came upon Mustela? What if they got lost as they searched?* His mind was a mess.

Phoebe thought for a moment. "They'll wonder where we've gone, back at the Lodge," she said. "Before we do anything, we need to let Grandfather know what's happened. And with Mustela on our backs, we should take extra precautions. We'd better get back."

"Well!" the old mouse squeaked as he saw them coming up the path. "I thought a snake had gotten you. Is your Magic Bird easily repaired?"

"It's gone, Grandfather," Phoebe replied.

"Gone?"

"We went to the spot, the exact spot, and it's just not there," said Sammy.

"The Magic Bird, gone?" Osmund blinked. "Mustela?"

"Who else?"

Osmund sat on a stone and thought. "Well…

there may be others who want it. Crows love shiny objects."

"That's possible."

"Or perhaps a human found it. There have been sightings of humans in the area recently."

"Hank!" Sammy squeaked excitedly. "Maybe Hank has come looking for me!"

Osmund nodded. "I'll send out some scouts to see if humans were nearby last night. But I still think it was Mustela."

"I'm sure Mustela can't fly it," said Sammy. "Not without me."

"Once Mustela discovers that *he* can't fly it," Phoebe said, "he'll want the one creature who *can*. That puts Sammy in danger."

Sammy wasn't deterred. "First he'll need to get the plane repaired. I bet even the great Mustela can't do that."

Osmund spoke solemnly. "True. The only one who might know the ins and outs of repairing the *Spirit* is Goggles."

Sammy cocked his head. "Who?"

"Goggles. A raccoon, older than dirt, like me. Wiser than wise. More clever than any of us by far. You should go talk to him. Maybe he's heard tell of where it is. Maybe Mustela and his gang brought it to him. He may know something, at any rate."

"Well, where is Goggles?" asked Sammy.

"I haven't seen hide nor hair of Goggles in a crow's age," replied Osmund. "And I couldn't say for sure where he lives now. He used to live in an old hollow tree about a day's journey west of here. Don't know if he still does."

"I remember, Grandfather," Phoebe said. "We went together, you and I, moons and moons ago. His den was…well, let's just say he's amazing, but kind of a recluse. Grandfather and Goggles were childhood friends, Sammy," she added.

"Ah, yes, a long time ago," Osmund said. "He was brilliant even then, always finding things, human objects mostly; collected every kind of doodad and gizmo you can imagine. Remarkable!"

"Then you know the way to find Goggles?" Sammy asked Phoebe.

"Well," Phoebe replied, "it's been a while, but I could probably get you there."

Osmund turned to Phoebe, his expression serious. "I'd rather you didn't venture away from the Lodge, Phoebe, with Mustela possibly lurking about."

Phoebe bristled. "No weasel is going to dictate what I do!" she said sharply.

"Granddaughter, he's capable of anything—believe me. I've seen Mustela bite through the spine of a young rabbit he was displeased with, as though it was nothing. He is quite ruthless, I can tell you that. You're to stay here."

Sammy shivered.

"Grandfather, I am perfectly capa—"

"You are to stay here!" Osmund said again. "End of discussion!"

Phoebe rolled her eyes.

The tall trees loomed overhead. Sammy imagined a day's journey through them and a

night in the wilds alone. He wasn't sure how to find Goggles; getting lost was a very real possibility.

"You *should* travel with someone who knows the Woods," Osmund said to Sammy. "Take someone from the Lodge with you. Phoebe can tell you what she remembers about the route."

Having a companion was a welcome thought, but then Sammy considered Mustela. "I don't think so," he said. "I'd be afraid of endangering anybody who comes with me."

"The Woods can be a dark and forbidding place," Osmund replied. "You must keep your wits about you at all times." He sighed. "I am sorry that we are not of more help to you. But now I must go rest my bones." He smiled at Sammy and Phoebe thoughtfully, then toddled up the path.

Sammy looked off into the Woods. He trembled, from both fear and anger. Someone had taken his *Spirit*, his connection to Hank and his way home. It felt personal. And Mustela had threatened Osmund and Phoebe, who had taken him in, sheltered and fed him, and who were being so kind.

"It's settled," he announced. "I'll go find Goggles. Alone. Maybe he'll know what happened to the *Spirit*. Along the way, I'll ask anybody and everybody I meet if they saw something or heard something or smelled something. I'll put the clues together and get my airplane back."

Phoebe clenched her paws. "This is crazy. Do you know anything about surviving here? Getting around? Finding food? I want to go with you. I know my way. I could help you, but

Grandfather has me under house arrest. He's such a worrywart."

"Well, I'm glad of it," Sammy said. "You'll be safer here."

"Won't you take someone else with you? A guide? Someone who knows the woods?"

Sammy looked at her seriously, then took a deep breath. "Thank you. I wish I could. But I told you: I don't want anyone taking risks on my account. I'm leaving in the morning. Alone."

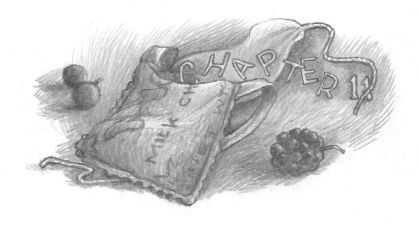

Early the next morning Sammy packed some seeds and berries and set off in the direction that Osmund had pointed: west.

At first he felt a thrilling sense of adventure and independence as he scampered down the old trail. But the farther he got from the lively bustle of the Lodge, the more quiet and immense and lonely the Woods felt. He had never been alone before, except for his flight in the *Spirit*. Now he was really on his own.

The trees seemed to stretch higher as he traveled the small, seldom-used path, casting deeper shadows and blocking more of the sky. Colorful butterflies fluttered by every now and then, but they only distracted him for a moment before the dark green gloom of the Woods took over again. He heard birdcalls, startling and sharp, and occasional insects humming, but mostly just vast silence.

A part of Sammy wished he had accepted Osmund's suggestion that he bring someone with him. He needed all the help he could get, and the companionship would have been a pleasant distraction. But he couldn't put another mouse in danger just for his own comfort. No, he'd do this on his own.

The day was still a seedling when he passed around the base of an enormous beech tree. After he climbed over several large, gray roots and made his way around the tree, he noticed that the path forked: one trail meandered west, the other zigzagged east.

"Oh, great. Now what?" he said out loud. "Which way?"

"You look lost," a voice croaked, and Sammy whirled around to find a large crow sitting on one of the tree roots.

"Oh!" Sammy squeaked. "I didn't see you."

"You look lost," the bird said again. "Are you?"

Sammy studied the bird carefully, deciding that it was probably more friend than foe. "Well, I thought I was fine, but this trail split, and now I'm not sure which way to go."

"I've heard that way's pretty nice," the crow replied, yawning and nodding toward the left. "But that way is, too," he added, tipping his beak to the right. "At least, so I've heard."

"You mean you're not sure?"

"Nah. Never been down either trail."

"Why not?"

"Can't fly."

"How come?"

"Broken wing."

"What happened?"

"Long drop."

"From where?" Sammy asked.

The crow pointed his beak up. "Fell out of the nest. Way up in this tree."

Sammy looked up into the beech. It was very tall; the branches above were a blur of green.

"That must have been awful."

"Serves me right for leaning too far over the edge."

Sammy glanced around. "How do you get enough to eat?"

"Oh," the crow said despondently, "I can

walk all right. I get by. But I would love to fly...just once."

"Gee." Sammy looked in his tote bag. "You want some raspberries?" he asked.

The crow gave Sammy a gloomy look. "Are you sure you want to waste them on me?"

"Sure." Sammy extended his paw. "Try these."

The crow plucked out two of the berries, tossed his head back, and swallowed them whole. "Thanks."

Sammy watched the crow for a moment. "So you say you want to fly someday?" he asked.

The crow nodded. "It's always been a dream of mine. But I don't see how it could ever happen."

"You know," Sammy said, "I think you'd just about fit in the *Spirit*."

"The what?"

"The *Spirit*."

"What's that?

"My airplane."

"You're nuts."

"You could fly!"

"Yeah, right."

"Above the trees!"

"Me. Fly."

"One problem."

"That figures."

"I don't know where the *Spirit* is," Sammy said. "I crash-landed some distance from here, and the next day it was missing. Someone took it. I'm looking for a raccoon named Goggles. I heard he might be able to help. I don't know if he'll know anything. But I've got to find him."

The crow looked skeptical, but he leaned forward to learn more. "This thing...this *Spirit*. What exactly are we talking about here?"

Sammy did his best to explain all about the wonders of an airplane.

"And you think, once you find it, I'll be able to fly?"

"That's exactly what I'm thinking. We could take to the air, with me at the controls, and you in the back. Trouble is, I've got this character Mustela on my back."

The bird's feathers fluffed up and he gave a little squawk. "Mustela? Why'd you have to mention him?"

"So you know him?"

"Who doesn't? Just my luck to have Mustela involved. He's one big meanie, to be avoided. I'd leave well enough alone if I were you."

"But just imagine: we're on the *Spirit*, you're flying high above the Woods, the wind in your face, Mustela far below…"

The crow cocked his head, and his eyes brightened. "Flying, huh? The wind in my…. Well…what have I got to lose?"

Sammy looked at the two trails that forked to the left and right. He made a decision. "This way!" he said.

And with that the two new friends set off.

CHAPTER 12

"What's your name?" Sammy asked.

"Everyone calls me Nose-Dive, for obvious reasons," the crow sighed. "But I prefer Blackie."

"Pleased to meet you, Blackie. I'm Sammy."

"You're not from around here, are you?" the crow asked.

Sammy chuckled. "No," he said, and then he told his story again, from beginning to end.

"I guess we've both sort of crash-landed," Blackie sighed again.

They walked and walked, always keeping an

eye open for any sign of the *Spirit*. As the day wore on they got hungry; the remaining bits in Sammy's knapsack had been eaten. Sammy found some tiny seeds to nibble, but nothing else looked familiar, and his stomach growled.

Blackie was lucky to spot an enormous earthworm that had been crossing the pathway, and he gobbled it up.

"I don't know how you can eat those," Sammy said.

"They're delicious," Blackie replied. "Look!

There's another one!"
He snapped at some-
thing cloaked beneath
some wild ginger leaves.

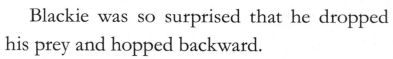

"Ouch!" a tiny voice
shrieked. "Stop that!"

Blackie was so surprised that he dropped
his prey and hopped backward.

A small, reddish creature popped out from
the leaves, thrashing in pain and clutching the
end of its tail. "Are you *crazy*?" it yelled. "That
hurt!"

"Gee…sorry!" Blackie apolo-
gized. "I never had a worm talk
back at me before."

"I am not a *worm*, you feath-
ered ignoramus. I'm a *newt*. A
very *irritated* newt, thanks to
you." The newt rubbed its tail

127

and looked Sammy and Blackie up and down. "Well, now that you've practically injured me for life, tell me: what are you two lamebrains doing here?"

"I...we...are looking for something," Sammy said. "A dark green airplane. Have you seen any sign of it?"

The newt frowned. "A what? Never heard of it. Saw some deer a while back, tromping through like they owned the place."

Sammy brightened. "Deer?" he asked. "How many? Were they carrying an airplane?"

The newt glared at Sammy. "Do you think I was busy

counting 'em? Are you *crazy?* I scrambled out of the way as soon as I heard 'em coming so the big klutzes wouldn't step on me. And like I said fifty times, I haven't seen any—any of whatever it is you're looking for!"

"An airplane. I'm just asking," Sammy said. "I was hoping maybe you saw some sign of it. I flew the airplane, but it crashed not too far from here."

"*You* flew," the newt said sarcastically.

"Yep."

"*Sure* you did."

"My airplane is called the *Spirit of Sammy.* I'm Sammy. And we're searching for it—and a raccoon named Goggles. I've been told he might know where to look for the *Spirit.* And hopefully how to repair it."

"Hmm." The newt still looked dubious.

"You know, Sammy," Blackie said. "Another

set of eyes might help us find where Goggles lives."

"Great idea!" Sammy looked at the newt. "You're welcome to join us if you like."

"As if I don't have better things to do than go gallivanting around the forest with *you* boneheads," the newt grumbled. "So that you can *fly*."

"Well, if you'd rather not…," said Sammy.

"Didn't say that," the newt replied grudgingly. "Just have lots to do today, that's all. But if you're *that* desperate for help, I guess I could come along, for a little while anyway."

Sammy smiled. "Great!" he said. "By the way, this is Blackie."

"Pleasure," the newt mumbled, half extending a foreleg. "Grace."

"Your name is Grace?" Sammy asked.

"Yeah…Grace. As in Grace*ful*. Now shut your hairy trap and let's get going."

Sammy and Blackie exchanged glances as they led the way down the trail. Grace kept up the pace, asking curt questions about the *Spirit* and how it came to be in the Woods to begin with.

"So you really think you're going to fly back. Back to where the humans live."

"If I can, if I ever find the *Spirit*," Sammy replied. "I'd like to get back home."

"Hmph." Grace rolled her eyes.

They stopped frequently, examining broken fern fronds and overturned stones, squinting high into the trees, looking for signs. Evening shadows drew quickly around them, and the three new friends decided to stop for the night.

"This looks like a good place." Blackie pushed into a thick clump of royal fern fronds, wiggling and fluffing and making a nice nest.

"You're sleeping there?" Grace asked bluntly. "Aren't you supposed to be getting your forty winks up in a tree somewhere?"

"I'm used to this," he remarked. "Every night." He tucked his beak under one of his wings and closed his eyes.

Grace continued. "Now that I think of it,

how come you're not up in the air, doing a search for the *Spirit?*"

"Blackie can't fly, Grace," Sammy said as he burrowed in next to the crow and nestled into his black feathers. It was nice to have the warmth next to him. He curled contentedly into a ball.

"Can't fly, huh?" Grace grunted. "How come? Afraid of heights? Hey! Make some room, for cryin' out loud! You're *hogging* it all!"

Sammy and Blackie scooted and shifted and made room for the newt. "Blackie's wings don't work so well, Grace," Sammy whispered quietly. "That's good for us, because he can keep us company here on the ground."

Grace, for once, had no comment.

Soon darkness had fallen, and the crickets lulled them to sleep.

The moon seemed to have just touched the tallest treetops when a scuffling noise woke them. The noise got closer.

"Do you hear that?" Sammy whispered.

"Yep," Blackie whispered back.

"What is it?"

"Don't know."

"Wanna look?"

"No way!"

"Me either."

"Will you two be *quiet?*" Grace groused. But in the light from the moon, Sammy saw that her eyes were wide with apprehension.

A tiny snorting, sniffing nose burst through the fern fronds, pointy and curious. It belonged to a diminutive shrew, who began to explore every inch of each nook and niche of their nest.

"Hey!" shrieked Grace. "What are you *doing?* Get *out* of here! You're invading my space!" She pulled off a bit of frond and gave the shrew a few thwacks.

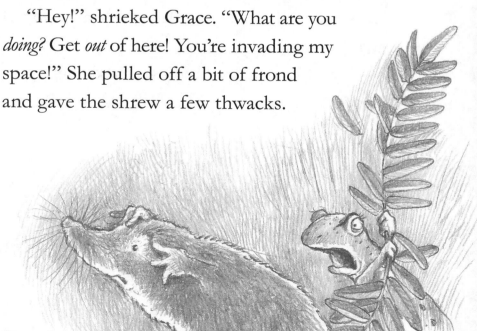

"Grace!" warned Sammy.

"But—it might eat us!" Grace hollered.

"Stay calm!" Blackie cawed out.

The shrew retreated a bit, still sniffing and snorting.

"Well, well!" it said cheerfully. "How's everybody this evening? Where's dinner?"

"We were asleep," Sammy said. "What is it you want?"

"Uh…just out grabbing a bite to eat," the shrew replied. "Sorry to disturb. Won't happen again. Night, folks."

The shrew started to leave, then wriggled back into the ferns. "You folks wouldn't have

a little snack to share, would you? Just a bite of something?"

"No, we wouldn't," Grace snipped. "Just who do you think you are?"

"Sorry," the shrew answered. "Hungry, that's all. Are you sure you don't have any spare worms...beetles...grasshoppers...caterpillars?"

"Hmph!" Grace muttered. "Freeloader!"

"Wish we had something for you," Sammy said. "As you can see, we're traveling pretty light."

"Where're you good folks off to?" the shrew asked.

Sammy sighed as he started to tell the story again.

Grace interrupted with a yawn. "Can we continue this fascinating narrative in the morning?"

But the shrew listened closely as Sammy told him about life in his shoe box and Hank. "Fed peanuts and other delectable goodies day and night, without lifting a paw? Remarkable!" it commented. "I sure like the idea of breakfast in bed. How about you making my introductions to Hank?"

"I can't make any promises," Sammy replied. "But you're welcome to come along with us, if you like."

"Well, nothing ventured, nothing gained, I always say!" the shrew squealed, clapping his paws. "Count me in, brother! The name is Peewee, by the way."

Sammy made the rest of the introductions.

"Glad to meet you, Blackie. Glad to meet you, Grace." Peewee extended his paw.

"Pleasure's all yours." Grace yawned again.

"Thanks for waking us up in the middle of the night."

"Sincerest apologies, Grace," replied Peewee. "Oh—there goes my stomach growling again. I wonder if there's something to snack on nearby...."

Grace rolled her eyes. "The guy is a bottom-less *pit*."

Sammy looked up. The sky was just beginning to brighten. The night had been a short one; dawn had arrived. "Let's go," he suggested. "A new day, with new places to search for the *Spirit*."

"Oh, brother," Grace sighed. "I hate morning mice."

Sunlight streamed through the understory and made dappled patterns on the Woods floor. Sammy was exhilarated by the fresh smells of the earth and the excitement of adventure. The challenge of finding the *Spirit* weighed on him. He wasn't sure where he was going, but he was happy to have the company of Blackie, Grace, and Peewee.

"Good morning," a voice called out from the side of the path.

Sammy was startled to see red eyes peering out from between the leaves. "Good morning!" he replied.

"A turtle," Grace grumbled. "Ignore him, or else he'll want to join us. And they go slow."

"Let's just stop and say hello," Sammy said.

The turtle dragged its heavy shell into the path. "Beautiful day, eh? Out for a stroll? Mind if I tag along?"

Grace groaned. "See what I mean?"

Sammy smiled. "Yes, beautiful day," he agreed. "We'd love the company, but to be honest we're in a bit of a hurry. So if you don't mind, we'll just scoot al—"

The turtle interrupted. "In a hurry, huh? Yessiree, seems like folks are always in a hurry these days. Me, I like to take my time. Name's Terrance, by the way."

"Stop and smell the roses, I always say," Peewee chimed in.

"Yep," Terrance added. "The roses, the

dandelions, the honey-
suckle, the pink clover,
the...."

Grace grimaced. "Oh,
brother, here we go."

"Hey Sammy," Blackie said.
"Maybe Terrance knows something about
Goggles's whereabouts."

"Excellent thinking, Blackie. Terrance, have
you heard of someone named Goggles?"

"Oh, yes," the turtle replied. "Smarty-pants
raccoon. Thinks he knows everything. Always
collecting junk like some sort of pack rat."

"That's got to be the same raccoon we're
looking for, Sammy," Peewee said.

Sammy nodded. "Do you know where he
lives? And how to get there from here?"

"Yep, could take you there myself,"

answered Terrance. "Follow me!" He started off, slowly scraping one foot in front of the other.

"Is this guy out of what's left of his mind?" moaned Grace. "We'd be better off walking backwards!"

"Uh, thanks, just the same," Sammy said. "But we'll be moving along."

"Suit yourself."

"Which way is it, did you say?"

"Follow this trail until you come to a creek. Cross the creek, but stay on the trail. Can't miss the giant tree that Goggles lives in. Don't fall down any rabbit burrows!" He chuckled.

They had headed up and around a hillside when Peewee asked, "When do we eat?" He sniffed the air in circles, hoping to detect the scent of some morsel or another. "I could sure use a great big juicy grub right about now. Sprinkled with snail eggs. Mmm-mmm!" He closed his eyes, rapturous. "Or maybe a nice bark beetle...crunchy on the outside, creamy on the inside...."

"Don't you ever think about anything but food?" Grace asked.

"I'm a growing boy," Peewee said sheepishly.

"What's the point of eating?" Blackie sighed. "You're just going to get hungry all over again."

"Yeah, but in the meantime you can enjoy it." Peewee grinned.

"Let's keep moving," Sammy said. "If we're ever going to find the *Spirit*, we have to keep looking, not standing here thinking about food."

"Over here!" Blackie called out. "Here's something!" He hunched over a long earthworm,

his toes resting across it. The earthworm wriggled and writhed but couldn't escape.

"The early bird catches the worm, I always say!" Peewee commented. "And just look at it! Oh, my! Pink and pretty and juicy and still wiggly! What are you guys going to eat?"

They stared at the shrew.

"What?" he asked.

"Don't you think we should share?" Sammy asked.

"Uh…oh, yeah," said Peewee. "Of course. Share and share alike, I always say."

As hungry as he was, Sammy couldn't quite choke down an earthworm slice. "You three can eat it. Divide it into thirds." He thought a moment. "Grace, you get first pick."

"Me? Oh! Thanks." Grace looked surprised. "I've never gone first before."

Peewee gobbled his piece before the others had even taken a bite.

"Nice job of sharing, everybody," Sammy said.

Peewee looked pleased. "Yeah," he agreed. "Nice job of sharing."

Sammy smiled. The little group was becoming a family.

After a little while they came to a stream. It wasn't very deep, but it was wide, and the water gurgled and rippled over thousands of smooth stones. Sammy had never seen water like this before. It looked treacherous.

"I guess we have to cross," he shouted over the rushing current. "Goggles must live somewhere on the other side. What'll we do?"

But Blackie was already in the water.
"Ooooh! Feels good!" he cawed. He waded into
a shallow eddy and fluttered his wings, dipping
them into the cool water and splashing drops
in all directions. "Wheee! This is great!"

"Blackie is actually smiling," Sammy remarked. "I didn't know he could!"

"Haw haw haw! Yippee!" Blackie laughed. "You should come in, too!" Water flew from his flapping wings, spraying everyone.

"Hey! Stop it, you maniac!" shouted Grace.

That was all Blackie needed to hear. He flicked his wings with gusto, spraying cascades of water at the bank and drenching Sammy and the others.

"Wha—?" Grace blinked in disbelief.

"If you can't beat 'em, join 'em, I always say!" Peewee scurried into the stream, splashing water at Blackie.

Laughing, Sammy lunged into the shallows and added to the mayhem. A full-blown water fight ensued.

153

After a moment, even Grace took part in the fun.

"Hey!" Blackie cawed out gleefully. "No fair! Three against one!"

"You started it!" Peewee laughed.

"And you're the biggest!" added Sammy.

"I'm soaked!" Blackie shrieked.

"Cleanliness is next to godliness, I always say!" Peewee snorted.

Soon the splashing contest was over, with everyone declaring him- or herself the winner. But the problem of crossing the creek still faced them.

"Osmund didn't mention this." Sammy contemplated the distant shore. "I can't swim."

Blackie wasn't fazed. "Not a problem," he said. His mood had changed. His voice was different, more genial. He gestured to his back. "Climb on board. The water isn't that deep. I can wade across; you three get to ride."

"Um, okay," Sammy said. "If you think you can hold all of us. Just start slowly and come back to the shore if you have any trouble."

Blackie crouched low. "Easy. Hop on, everybody."

Sammy, Grace, and Peewee scrambled up and sat astride the glossy blue-black back of the crow as he eased into the flowing stream.

"Go slowly, Blackie," Sammy cautioned. "It's a little bouncy back here."

"Just hold onto my feathers. You'll be fine!" Blackie hollered over his shoulder.

"Now who would have thought I'd ever be riding across a river on the back of a bird?" Grace called out.

"A sound mind makes for a sure foot, I always say," Peewee said. "I…I hope Blackie doesn't slip!"

"Hang on tight!" Blackie yelled above the sound of the rushing water. "We've got some rapids coming up!"

The three friends gripped feathers and each other, as Blackie tiptoed his way carefully across the stream. The stones under his feet were smooth and slippery, and the current got stronger.

Suddenly they heard a voice from the shore behind them, calling out above the din of the rapids.

"Sammy! Wait!"

"Phoebe! Am I glad to see you!" Sammy squealed. He hopped off Blackie's back as the crow neared shore again, then he grabbed Phoebe's paws, shaking them vigorously. "What happened? What are you doing here?"

"I couldn't bear the thought of you in the Woods, alone. I had a feeling you might need me." She glanced at the little group. "But it looks like you found help. I've been following your trail...and you certainly leave one!"

"Yes, well.... Wait, does Osmund know you've joined us?" Sammy asked.

Phoebe looked a little embarrassed. "I slipped away from the Lodge. Let's just say I haven't told him yet."

"Phoebe!"

"I know. I should have, but then he would have never let me go."

"He's going to be plenty sore at you."

"Yes, I know he will be." She looked at the little group questioningly.

Sammy grinned. "These kind folks have been helping me look for the *Spirit*. This is Blackie. He was just about to get us across this water. Very bravely, I should add."

"Oh, I dunno...." Blackie blushed.

"And this is Grace, who has really kept our spirits up."

"Ah, well, no big deal. Just doing my part," Grace said.

"And this is Peewee."

Peewee looked expectantly at Sammy.

"Uh, Peewee is the very best at finding food, and sharing it," Sammy said.

Peewee beamed. "A chain is only as strong as it weakest link, I always say!"

"And this is Phoebe. Osmund's grand-daughter and Future Queen."

Everyone's eyes widened. "W-wow," stuttered Blackie.

"Happy to know all of you," Phoebe said. "Friends of Sammy's are friends of mine." She turned to Sammy. "Any luck finding the *Spirit?*"

"None yet."

"That's too bad."

Sammy looked determined. "But we're still heading west. Still looking for Goggles. Osmund said he was about a day's journey, so we should be close."

"Look," Phoebe said. "I recognize this area.

There's no need to cross the creek. Goggles's tree is on this side. We should be close."

"Good. But I want to get you back to the Lodge. Mustela may be looking for us. You could be in danger."

"Maybe Mustela's got the *Spirit*," offered Grace.

Phoebe chuckled. "Oh, we'd have heard about it if he did, Grace. He'd be gloating and bragging. Sammy, I'm not going back to the Lodge. I came here to help…let's go find Goggles."

A strange buzzing sound filled the air.

Blackie gave a little croak of alarm, and his feathers ruffled. "What's that?" he asked.

They all stood silently, ears cocked.

"Sounds like a beehive," said Grace.

"Or a flock of birds," suggested Peewee.

They listened intently for a moment, ears

cocked to the sky. Then Sammy's eyes widened with excitement. "It's the *Spirit!*" he shouted. "It's far off, but I think it's getting closer!"

"Are you sure?" asked Phoebe. "I can hardly hear it. It's so faint."

"It's the *Spirit*, and I bet Hank is coming, too. Good ol' Hank!"

The sound seemed to be coming not from above the trees, but through them. And as it got closer, it became clear that what they were hearing was not the buzzing of a plane, but rather the squeaks and humming of…something else.

"Sounds kind of creepy," Blackie whispered.

"It's getting louder," Peewee said softly. "I don't like this."

They turned and looked up through the tree canopy just as a swarm of flying creatures descended upon them like flies on a carcass,

a dizzying hoard of flapping wings that criss-crossed, flipped, dipped, and turned, sounding like hundreds of snapping twigs. Their high-pitched squeaks added to the confusion.

"Whadda we do?" cawed Blackie.

"Everybody, run for cover!" Phoebe shouted. "Hide! Anywhere!"

Peewee dove under some leaf litter, finding an old mole tunnel and digging in. Grace wiggled under a slab of bark, curled into a ball, and peeked out.

The flying creatures surrounded Blackie, who stabbed and pecked at the swooping mass until he found cover under a low hemlock bough.

Sammy froze in panic, unable to move as the creatures descended from the sky and landed all around them.

"Sammy! Here!" Phoebe shouted. She grabbed him and they darted under a large mushroom.

"W-what are they?" Sammy asked.

"They're voles," Phoebe whispered back. "But flying voles. Voles...somehow with wings!

The wings of bats! I've never seen anything like it!"

"But why are they here?"

"I have a bad feeling about this," Phoebe said. "Stay still. Don't even blink."

They felt the vibrations as the flapping wings swooped overhead. The wild squeaking continued as one vole after another flew just above the forest floor.

Then they heard another voice, darker and deeper. Phoebe peeked out from beneath the toadstool cap. "Sammy!" she gasped. "It's him!"

Mustela hung in the air a few feet above them shouting out a series of commands. Huge dark

brown wings were attached to his shoulders
with leather straps.

"Find him!" Mustela commanded. "He's

here somewhere! Hiding! Under a leaf! A piece of bark! Find him!"

Sammy felt a chill as though his whole body had been dipped in ice water. Mustela was referring to him! The swarm of flying voles was a search party, and Sammy was the prize. And his tail was poking out from the edge of the toadstool cap, the tiniest tip of pink, barely noticeable. Sammy flicked it under the mushroom cap.

The weasel's keen eyes spotted the movement. "There!" he shrieked, gestering at the toadstool.

Sammy and Phoebe exchanged a panicky glance. "What do we do?" Sammy squeaked.

"Go, fast!" Phoebe sputtered. "Run!"

The two mice darted and leaped over branches and fallen debris as fast as their legs could move. They zigzagged and crisscrossed,

feigning left turns and right turns, trying des-
perately to outmaneuver the swarm of flying
voles.

"Let's split up!" Phoebe called out. "Harder
to catch the two of us if we do!"

The two friends immediately careened in opposite directions, causing several voles to collide with one another. Sammy had never moved so fast before, and his heart beat furiously as he avoided the grasping claws of the flapping minions above him.

Over, around, and under fern fronds, piles of leaves, clumps of fungi, and patches of emerald moss, he dodged and swerved and doubled back, the ground beneath him a blur of brown and green.

Vole after vole swooped down. Suddenly several of them tackled him. Sammy felt their claws on his back, and a moment later he was wrenched aloft.

He heard Phoebe's frantic cry below. "Sammy!"

Looking down as he rose into the air, he saw Phoebe peek out from her hiding place, her eyes terrified.

"Phoebe! Phoebe! Help!" he squeaked. Then he was carried above the dogwoods and spice-bush and even higher, until the mist-covered crowns of the giant oaks and pines and poplars hid the ground from view.

Sammy nibbled on some sunflower seeds, relishing the dark coziness of his shoe box. He smiled to himself as he curled up into a ball and nestled into the sweet-smelling sawdust.

But the smell: was that sawdust…or wood smoke?

He jerked out of his dream to the sound of voices shrieking and laughing. He remembered now. He'd been in the Woods…looking for the *Spirit*.… Where were his new friends? Where was Phoebe?

His head was throbbing. He tried to lift

his paws but found he couldn't: he was bound tightly with honeysuckle vine. His mouth was stuffed with a dirty rag.

In a rush he remembered the attack of the voles, the terrifying trip above the treetops in their tight clutches, the tall figure of Mustela, grinning arrogantly.

Sammy shivered. It had not been a dream.

Night had blanketed the Woods. Light from a campfire eerily lit the misty gloom. Giant oaks and pines towered above him like fortress walls.

There was another burst of raucous laughing. Sammy's head quickly cleared as he saw a group of rats gathered around a haphazardly constructed campfire. The winged voles hung back, clustered together in the shadows, their eager faces lit by the firelight.

Embers rolled dangerously close to the leaves and pine needles on the forest floor. None of the rats seemed to notice or care. They were seated around the fire eating and drinking; several of them passed acorn cap mugs of frothy liquid back and forth. In between two of the rats sat Mustela. Sammy watched as the two rats removed Mustela's wing harness. His fur glistened, sleek and smooth.

"Quiet, quiet," he commanded as he jumped up on a log. "I'd like to say a few words, with your indulgence." He grinned, showing his pointy teeth.

"It has been a most rewarding day. We have captured someone who can teach me to fly the Magic Bird."

The crowd erupted into high-pitched hurrahs. Some danced rat-jigs and others yanked

each other's tails. Two rats raised flaming twigs and poked at each other in a mock sword fight.

Mustela grinned at the fireside scene, one paw on his hip, the other cunningly stroking his long dark whiskers. He raised his arms, and the group quieted.

"Of course we all covet the Magic Bird," he said. "There must be magic within it that we can only dream of. Who knows where that magic can take us? Power and prestige, ruling the entire Woods…and beyond. And this"—he gestured at Sammy—"this brings us one step closer to finding it."

Sammy's eyes widened. *They don't have it?* he thought. *Then they must think I know where it is. And I'll be in big trouble when they find out I don't.* In a panic, he began pulling and yanking at his bindings. But it was futile. He was tied fast.

"Here's the plan." Mustela's voice deepened. "Our captive mouse here knows the whereabouts of the Magic Bird. He'll never willingly tell us, of course, but we can try to make him talk."

Sammy squeaked and struggled again with the honeysuckle cords.

The rats cheered, their firelit eyes gleaming with anticipation. "How do we make him tell us?" one called out.

"This I haven't decided yet. One must be deliberate and thoughtful when selecting certain...procedures." Mustela stepped off of the log and rippled over to Sammy.

"If he doesn't disclose the whereabouts of the Magic Bird, I'm considering a simple, time-tested method: dropping him from a considerable height, courtesy of the flying voles.

But it's so dull! And over so quickly. One *splat* and it's done! No suspense!"

The rats guffawed and slapped each other's backs.

Sammy gasped, and wiggled frantically under the bindings.

"Or picture this: he's tied to a stake. A stake at the entrance of a rattlesnake's den!" He grabbed Sammy's tail and gave it a yank.

Sammy squeaked a muffled "Ouch!"

"Think of the delight, after the initial pounce and swallow, of watching this little pink tail disappear. And a lump that moves slowly, slowly, down, down, down...."

Squeaking with fear, Sammy continued to struggle as the rats pointed and snickered. The honeysuckle vine was tough and strong.

"Whatever method I decide, he'll have a day

or so to think it over first: talk, or face the con-sequences. Meanwhile, more festivities!"

Sammy watched, wide-eyed, as the celebra-tion continued into the night. The moon arced over the Woods. The orange and red embers of the fire had nearly burned out when one by one Mustela and the rats collapsed into their tents.

Through his daze, Sammy felt something nibbling at his tough honeysuckle straps, then recognized Phoebe's voice, barely audible.

"Quiet."

She gnawed and loosened the vines until Sammy could wiggle his paws and toes in and out. He tried to get the blood back into them, but his limbs were numb. He could barely move or stand. Phoebe pulled the rag from his mouth.

"How did you find me?" he whispered.

"Wasn't hard. We could hear the rats laughing and carousing all through the Woods. Then we followed the light of the campfire."

"Is everybody else all right?"

"Quiet," Phoebe whispered. "Everyone's fine." She put her arm around him, holding him steady until the blood returned to his toes. Then they disappeared into the darkness of the bracken.

The only noise that could be heard was the snoring of the rats and the cadence of the singing crickets.

CHAPTER 16

Only when they had gone a good distance from Mustela and the rats did they dare speak.

"I'm so happy to see you," Sammy whispered. "It's okay, I can walk now. How did you find me? Those horrible flying voles...."

"We followed them, saw the direction they were heading. The light and smell of the campfire helped. Are you all right?"

"Those crazy rats tied me up so tightly that I could barely move."

"Did they talk about the *Spirit*?"

"Yes. They don't have it! But they think *I do*—and they want it badly enough to torture me for it."

Just then, Blackie, Peewee, and Grace emerged out of the darkness. "Sammy!" Blackie croaked quietly. "You okay?"

"I'm fine—just glad to see you guys safe and sound!"

"And are we glad to see you!" Grace said. "We thought you were gone for good, but we never gave up."

Sammy smiled. "Well, I'm just glad you rescued me, and we're all together again. That was brave!"

"I was the one who smelled the campfire smoke first!" Peewee boasted, pumping Sammy's paw vigorously.

"You? It was me who saw the light from the campfire," Blackie said.

"Well, I was the one who suggested that it was Mustela's campfire," humphed Grace.

Phoebe sighed. "Look, everybody did their part in finding Sammy."

"That must have been quite a trip, way up there in the air," Blackie continued.

"You were so high!" squeaked Peewee. "We were the lookouts while Phoebe untied you."

"I was the lead lookout," Grace declared.

"I thought I was the lead lookout," Blackie cawed.

Phoebe rolled her eyes. "You were all lead lookouts. We've rescued Sammy. Now let's get out of here before Mus—"

Sammy interrupted. "We need to find the *Spirit* right away. Mustela doesn't have it. I vote we keep heading to Goggles's tree. He might have some clues."

"Sammy," Phoebe said. "I'm afraid I'm a little turned around, what with following the voles, the darkness…. I'm not sure I can find the way."

"How about west?" Peewee offered.

"Second that!" Grace agreed.

"Ditto!" said Blackie.

Sammy was silent. His arrival in the Woods had endangered his friends and their whole community. He wanted to see them safely home again, but he needed to find his plane if he was ever going to get home to Hank.

The sun was barely showing its first pale glow of dawn.

Sammy looked at his little band of friends, a stalwart and dedicated group. "All right. Which way is west, Phoebe?" he asked.

Phoebe pointed. "This way!"

"Anybody still want to go with me?" he asked.

"Let's go!" they all shouted, and they set off deeper into the Woods.

CHAPTER SEVENTEEN

The sun had risen a quarter of the way along its arc when they stumbled upon a pile of rock mostly covered with weeds, vines, and young trees. After cautiously exploring and sniffing about, they discovered that the rocks were the crumbling remnants of the walls of a stone house. The rusting metal roof had long ago collapsed; it now nestled in a bed of decay on the forest floor. The tottering remains of a chimney poked above the taller saplings like an aging sentinel.

Countless ants, termites, beetles, worms,

and fungi had done their job: the old wooden joists and beams and rafters were slowly decomposing. Everything was infused with the damp, pungent odor of wood, rot, and decay.

"What the heck is this?" Grace wondered out loud. "It looks kind of creepy."

"I'd say definitely human," Phoebe said. "And I agree, Grace. Creepy."

Sammy stopped, cocking his ears. "Listen! What's that?" he asked. "It's coming from inside. Wait here."

He cautiously climbed over what had once been a door stoop, then crawled under a section of the collapsed tin roof into a small space of crazy angles and pitched beams. Inside, he expected to see more signs of deterioration.

Instead he discovered that the room was alive.

Clocks ticked from every corner. Several

music boxes played, and a variety of wind-up toys beeped, rattled, or tweeted. A dented copper teakettle, heated by a small oil lamp, whistled. The air was filled with ringing, chiming, and ticking.

Tables and shelves were covered in parts and pieces of alarm clocks, lawnmower engines, electric mixer motors, lamps, doorknobs, pocket watches, baby carriage wheels, light switches, coffee percolators, and radios.

Books were piled on the floor and stacked on shelves. Some were tattered and damp and moldy; others were open and bookmarked to specific pages.

Every surface of the room was occupied. Every niche was filled.

A heavyset raccoon shuffled into the room carrying a small can of machine oil. His whiskers were gray, and his striped tail was losing

some of its fur, but his eyes sparkled behind a set of yellowed Bakelite goggles.

"That must be Goggles!" Sammy murmured to himself.

The raccoon was so absorbed in what he was doing that he didn't see Sammy standing in the doorway. He shuffled over to an open book on a table, tracing his paw down the pages and muttering to himself.

"Let's see. Engine oiled, check. Trim tab trimmed, check. Vertical stabilizer restabilized, check. New left aileron attached, check. Ooh, that was a doozie. Now where's my screwdriver?"

He wandered about the room opening tins and boxes, shaking jars and crocks, and poking through piles.

"Ah, good. Here it is. Presto!" He pulled a

wooden-handled screwdriver out of an old tin can full of parts.

He was turning to leave the room when he finally discovered Sammy and flinched in surprise. "Who are you?" he barked. "What do you want?"

"H-hello," Sammy said. "My name is Sammy Shine."

"Oh? Sammy, did you say?"

"Yes, sir."

"Well? What are you doing here?"

"Are you Goggles?"

"That's my name."

"I've come a long way to find you."

"Me? Is that so? Why?"

Sammy opened his mouth to answer, but just then there was a scrambling noise at the doorway. Phoebe, Blackie, Peewee, and Grace were peering in.

"What is this?" Goggles asked. "State your business."

"These are my friends, sir," Sammy said.

Phoebe extended a paw. "I'm Phoebe. You may not remember, but I visited you many moons ago with my grandfather, Osmund."

"Oh? Ah, yes! Of course I remember you, Phoebe." Goggles grinned.

"I remember you lived in a tree then," Phoebe said, gazing around the room. "You live here now?"

The raccoon chuckled. "Yes, outgrew the old place. Needed more room for my gadgets."

"Grandfather sends his greetings," Phoebe added.

"Ah! And how is Osmund? In good health, I hope?"

"He is well, thank you."

Blackie clacked his bill nervously. "Hello!" he cawed. "I'm Blackie."

Goggles nodded. "Nice to meet you, Blackie."

"And I'm Grace." The newt bowed low, fidgeting with her red tail. "Interesting place you have here!"

"Thank you, Grace."

"And this is Peewee," Sammy said.

Peewee tingled with nervous excitement.

"H-hello!" he giggled. "Glad to meet you!"

"Thank you, Peewee." Goggles turned to Sammy. "Well," he said. "I don't ordinarily allow visitors into my workshop. Especially a crowd."

Sammy looked at his little group of friends. "I'm sorry to intrude, Goggles," he said. "But we need your help."

"Perhaps you should tell me what brings you to this remote part of the Woods, Sammy."

"I was in an airplane, flying it, and it crashed here in the Woods," Sammy began. "It was a beautiful airplane called the *Spirit of Sammy*— named after me! And then I met Phoebe here, and her grandfather…and then Mustela started to threaten everyone, and then there were flying voles, and I got captured, and they were going to torture me to find out where the plane was, but even if I had talked, what could I say?

It had vanished from the last place I saw it! But then these guys rescued me. And...."

Suddenly Sammy was overwhelmed by the events of the last few days. He looked blankly at Phoebe.

"We've been searching for you," she told Goggles. "We were hoping that you might know where to look for the *Spirit*, or maybe know what happened to it. And, since it needed repairs, that you might help us fix it. You're our only hope."

A wide grin stretched across the old raccoon's mouth. "Airplane, huh?" he asked. "I've heard tell of airplanes. Been fascinated with them ever since I was a little pollywog. Amazing inventions, airplanes, don't you think? Well, you may be interested in a little something I've got out back."

Goggles led the way
to the rear of his workshop
and out an opening under the collapsed
tin roof. The backyard was strewn with
another assortment of parts and pieces, only
larger: machinery parts, bits and pieces of old
furniture, crockery, rusted components of
various appliances.

And in the middle of the chaos sat the *Spirit*.

It was as gleaming and bright as if the crash had never happened. The wheels and landing gear looked repaired. The wing flaps seemed fixed. Everything was mended. The *Spirit* looked ready to take to the air.

Phoebe stared at the dark green airplane, awestruck. She poked Sammy. "Say something!" she whispered.

"It's the *Spirit!*" Sammy gasped. "And it looks like new! It's all fixed!" He turned to Goggles. "Did you do this?"

"Wasn't much to do, really. I had all the

parts I needed…you may have noticed I have large supply of used parts. So it was just a matter of fitting, cutting, patching. Quite a piece of machinery you have here, Sammy. A real gem. Whoever built this knew what he or she was doing. Fixing it was pure joy for me."

"How did you find it?" Sammy asked.

"Well, it wasn't hard to notice when the *Spirit* came to the Woods," Goggles said. "One could hear the noise from quite a distance. The engine sounded pretty sweet, and I just had to know what machine was making that roar. I followed my ears and didn't see any survivors. Then I thought maybe it was radio-controlled, with nobody on board. So I dragged it back here to see if I could put it right. It's quite a beauty."

Sammy ran his paws along the smooth

surface of the painted balsa. "I can't believe it," he murmured. "I just can't believe it. I'm going home! I'm going home! Can I fly it?"

Goggles grinned proudly. "Should run like a dream."

Sammy turned and looked at the group. "I miss Hank. But to get home to him, I'll have to leave my friends…and I'm not sure I can."

There was a rustling nearby, and a young skink scooted out from under the leaf litter. "I-I've come to warn you," he panted.

Goggles gave a start. "Warn me? Warn me about what?"

"About Mustela." The skink glanced around nervously, his tongue darting in all directions. "He's coming. Here. He wants the Magic Bird."

"How do you know?" Sammy asked.

"I was under a leaf, see. Minding my own business. Mustela walked by. Almost stepped on me! But didn't see me. I was hidden, you know? He says to one of his cronies, 'The only way I'll get that Magic Bird is to steal it from Goggles himself!' Then he says, 'I want a dozen of you rats to come with me. We'll leave today.' I heard it all. They're coming here!"

"How does Mustela know that I have the *Spirit?*" Goggles asked.

"You're the only one in the Woods who has the know-how to make it work again," Phoebe answered. "He thought of you, just like we did. Thank you so much," she said to the skink.

The skink flicked his tail. "Mustela's a bully. And I'm glad to help," he said proudly.

"I hope I can ask you to help us one more time. Please go find Osmund. Tell him that I am well, and that we found Goggles. And tell him that you're to be treated well."

"Thank you," the skink said. "I'll be off right away. And, well…bye!" He turned, tasting the air with his tongue, and then darted away into the snapdragons.

Goggles turned to the little group. "You are all in danger," he said, his tone serious. "You do know that Mustela will not treat any of you kindly after you've helped Sammy here." He looked at Phoebe. "You most of all."

"So what do we do?" Peewee squeaked.

"There's only one thing to do. You'll all be leaving. On the *Spirit*."

The little group stared at him.

Sammy grinned. "Of course! We'll all go!"

"Wow!" Peewee giggled.

"Will everybody fit?" Grace asked, glancing at Blackie.

Goggles pointed at the gas engine. "I think the *Spirit* is powerful enough to—"

"Wait!" Phoebe interrupted. "I can't just leave. What about my home...my life here? And Grandfather?"

Goggles nodded. "Yes, it's a difficult decision for you, my dear. But I'm afraid the alternative isn't a pleasant one. I can only imagine what Mustela has in mind for you."

"Come with us, Phoebe. You must!" encouraged Sammy.

Phoebe looked bewildered.

Goggles gave her a reassuring pat. "We have lots to do and little time," he said. "We need to prepare. Blackie, Sammy, Phoebe, look around here for rope and bring me whatever you find. Grace, Peewee, help me drag this fishing net outside. We must work together, and quickly!"

"Six heads are better than one, I always say!" Peewee hollered.

"What do you do, sit around making up corny sayings all day?" Grace groused.

It wasn't long before Goggles's plan had taken shape. A long rope hung over a branch near the entrance to the workshop. One end of it ran along the ground and disappeared under a camouflaging blanket of leaf litter. The other end was tied to an open fishing net, unnotice-able under a dusting of leaves and other debris.

When an unsuspecting prey stepped onto the net, Goggles could pull the other end of the rope and draw the net closed, trapping the target.

"I wish I had something...something that would be sure to lure Mustela into the trap," Goggles pondered.

Grace pointed to Sammy's flight helmet. "How about that?"

"Brilliant!" Sammy said. "Grace, thanks!"

Grace beamed.

"Necessity is the mother of invention, I always say!" Peewee chimed in.

"And we'll soon see how well our invention works," Goggles added. "Mustela is tough, but hopefully the net is tougher. Now...let's get the *Spirit* ready for takeoff!"

"Takeoff?" Sammy asked, surprised. "How can the *Spirit* take off from here?"

"I've got it all figured out," Goggles said. "Come with me."

They trooped around the side of the collapsed roof, and Goggles pointed up. "See that?" he asked. "That's your runway."

Sammy looked at the crumbled, collapsed metal roof. "What's a runway?"

"Didn't you have a runway before?" Goggles asked. "How did the *Spirit* get into the air?"

"Well...Hank's brother threw it."

"Hmm. I see. Well, we'll need a surface where the *Spirit* can take off without any obstructions," the raccoon explained. "Something flat and not too bumpy. According to my calculations, the roof is perfect." He put his paw to his chin, pondering, and then scooted off.

"What's Goggles talking about, Sammy?" Phoebe asked.

Sammy's eyes followed Goggles as he disappeared into his workshop. "I don't know," he answered. "I guess we'll find out."

Goggles emerged with Blackie and Peewee, carrying a long piece of sisal. "Somebody threw this away. Can't imagine why," he muttered to

himself. "Perfectly good...strong...just right for us."

"Just right for what?" Grace asked. "What are you going to do with that?"

"We are going to hoist the *Spirit* up to the top of the roof, using this rope," Goggles answered. "Then Sammy can use the roof as the runway, of course. I've calculated the slope, the angle, the distance—it should all work fine. It will help of course if the wind and weather cooperate."

"Uh, but how do we get the *Spirit* up there with a rope when we're all down here?" Peewee asked.

Goggles grinned. "Follow me," he said. He fastened one end of the rope to the tail of the *Spirit*, then organized the group into a line, paws on rope.

"If we're synchronized, this should be easy,"

Goggles said. "We'll pull the *Spirit* to the base of the roof, then up over the eave. That will be the tough part. Once it's up on the roof, we anchor it there. Okay, everyone. Ready?"

Sammy took a deep breath. "Okay, Goggles. We're ready!" he said.

"Pull!" Goggles barked.

The six of them took hold of the rope and pulled hard.

Goggles was old but tough and surprisingly strong.

Sammy and Phoebe were agile and fit.

Peewee was tiny, but what he lacked in size he made up for in gusto.

Grace was determined. She grabbed Peewee from behind and held on tightly.

At the rear Blackie held the rope in his beak, straining as he backed up, his claws scraping on the rusty tin roof.

"Pull!" Goggles commanded. "Pull!"

Inch by inch, the *Spirit* moved over the ground and up to the edge of the roof.

"Winners...never quit, and...quitters... never...win, I always say!" Peewee puffed.

Finally the wheels rolled up the smooth surface to the top of the tin roof. Sammy lashed the rope tightly to an old nail.

"We need one more thing." Goggles crawled back to his workshop, then reemerged with a partially filled can of motor oil. He balanced the can on the peak of the roof. "Whew!" he gasped. "Good work, everyone. I think now we're all set." He examined the rope and studied the sloping roof. "Yep. Looks like the *Spirit* is ready to take off. And our trap is set."

Though it was wonderful to see the *Spirit*, Sammy was nervous, realizing he would soon be behind the controls again, with the safety

of his friends in his hands. He hoped he hadn't forgotten what little he had learned the first time...and that Goggles had made all the right repairs.

The trip was risky. There was a lot to lose. Maybe life in the Woods, with his new family of friends, was the better option.

They all perched on the roof's ridge, lined up like sentinels.

"All we do now is wait," Sammy said.

They didn't have to wait long.

A moment later, they heard a shout from below.

Mustela and a squad of his rat cronies oozed their way through the grass and weeds around the ruins of the house. They seemed to be using their keen senses of smell to guide them, sniffing every stone, every rotting plank, and every twisted bit of rusty gutter, trying to pick up the scent of their prey.

"It's him," Grace mouthed.

"He hasn't seen us yet," Sammy whispered.

"But he's getting closer." Phoebe gestured to the net.

"Yes…Mustela," Goggles murmured grimly.

"Long time no see. Well, he's here. This is it. Everybody into the *Spirit*. Quietly if you can. I think the time has come for us to test our trap—and my airplane repair skills."

Sammy squirmed into the cockpit and Phoebe followed right behind. Peewee and Grace hopped into the baggage compartment as silently as they could.

"Come on, Blackie!" Peewee squeaked.

"Me too?" the crow asked.

"Of course, you too!" Grace whispered emphatically. "We've left room for you. Get in!"

Goggles poked his fuzzy nose into the cockpit window and spoke quietly. "When I say 'Now,' you pull the bar and rev the engine, remember? Then when you think the time is right, give Peewee the signal. You've got the strongest jaws, Peewee. Chew through the rope

a little bit here, and then when Sammy tells you, chew the rest of the way through. That'll set us free to take off. Understand?"

Peewee nodded, his eyes huge and serious. He wiggled his jaw back and forth to warm it up.

Goggles leaned over the edge of the roof and peered at the invading rats down below. Mustela was in the lead and was only steps away from the trap.

"He's almost there," whispered Goggles. He scrambled back to the airplane. "It looks like adventure ahead. I wish I could go with you."

"Thanks for everything, Goggles," Sammy said. "I...I hope you'll be okay!"

"I'll be fine." The old raccoon's eyes were moist behind the goggles. "Well then, I guess it's good luck, everyone!"

They heard Mustela shout. He had picked up Sammy's scent. The weasel stopped at the entrance of the workshop, pausing to bark an order. He spotted Sammy's helmet and slithered over to it, standing right in the middle of the camouflaged net.

Goggles yanked hard on the rope. In a flash the net scooped up Mustela, who thrashed wildly about, hissing and shrieking. His band of rat troopers could only stare, wide-eyed.

The net looked like it would rip apart any moment.

Goggles looked at the little group. "Everybody ready?"

"Ready!" they announced.

He scrambled over up to the propeller, placed his paws on one of the blades, and gave it a hard thrust.

Thwop!

The propeller turned, then stopped.

Goggles gave it another try.

Thwop!

Mustela wiggled in the net and turned to look up at the roof ridge. "There! There they are!" he shrieked. "Hurry! After them!"

The small army of rats surged up the roof, clawing at the metal surface.

Thwop! Thwop! Thwop!

Again and again Goggles jerked at the propeller. "Come on," he urged the engine. "I know you've got it in you!"

He thrust down onto the propeller another time. The engine sputtered and awoke.

"It's the Magic Bird!" Mustela shouted to the

rats. "Get it! Get them! Don't let it get away!"

Goggles tipped over the can of oil in Mustela's direction, spilling it down the sloping tin roof. The rats scrambled, slipping and scraping, piling upon one another again and again, then sliding down again as they attempted to reach the *Spirit*.

The *Spirit* roared to life, the sound of the engine filling the Woods. The tin roof vibrated. At the end of the rope, the plane strained to break free.

"Here goes!" Sammy cried out, his voice almost drowned out by the screaming engine. "Everybody hold on!" He tried to remember what he had done before. Tentatively he revved the throttle and the noise became even more deafening.

"Sammy!" Phoebe squeaked. "Maybe this is a bad idea!"

But it was too late for second thoughts. Sammy yelled out the little side window: "Now, Peewee, *now!*"

Peewee furiously chewed at the rope that held down the *Spirit*.

They could see the throng of rats struggling to scale the slippery roof. They were now building a rat pyramid.

"Come on, Peewee!" encouraged Grace. "Chew faster! You've almost got it!"

Peewee bit
through the last
of the sisal strands.
The rope snapped
and the plane jolted
forward. Peewee
dove on board, and
the *Spirit* started
down the sloping roof.

In a mouse's heartbeat, the plane had reached
the bottom of the slope and was flung into
the curved bend of the crumpled roof. It shot
out of the curve and, engine whining, raced
into the air.

"Goodbye! Goodbye! Happy landing!"
shouted Goggles. "Hmm," he added. "Landing...hadn't thought about landing!"

CHAPTER 20

The *Spirit* soared out and over the treetops. The propeller clipped through the tips of the highest leaves of a poplar, and a flurry of green bits rained down on Goggles, Mustela, and the rats.

"Watch it!" squealed Phoebe. "You're flying too close!"

But Sammy felt assured as he gripped the controls; it was all coming back to him. He banked the plane easily and steered it slowly and steadily in an upward lazy spiral, above the danger of the grasping trees. Then he squinted at the sky, judging his directions, and pointed the *Spirit* toward the south. Toward home. Toward Hank.

Grace watched as the scrambling rats on the roof below got farther and farther away. "We made it!" she squeaked. "We're *flying!*"

Peewee grinned. "Well, when the going gets tough, the tough get going, I always say!"

"I guess we're really leaving," Phoebe said.

Mesmerized, they gazed at the treetops below.

In a few minutes, they were over the edge of the Woods. A few moments more and they were sailing over open fields and meadows.

Everything—the sights, the vastness of the world, the exhilaration of it all—was astonishing.

"Look! There's the Woods, far behind us! And look there, way down! A black and white

deer!" Phoebe said.

Blackie's eyes filled with wonder. "I'm flying! I'm flying!" he cawed. The plane passed another crow, flying in the same direction.

"Hey, you!" Blackie screeched. "What a slowpoke! Get the lead out!"

Grace squealed with delight. "Whoever thought a newt could fly so high!"

Peewee clung to the edge of th compartment doorway. "I'm dizzy!" he squeaked. "We're so far up!"

243

"Then don't look down!" Grace hollered.

"But I can't help it!"

Sammy scanned the landscape below for anything familiar. They were passing over rolling pastures and cornfields. He spotted a small group of red roofs among a group of trees ahead. "There!" he called out to Phoebe. "That looks like home!"

"But how do we get down?" she shouted.

Before Sammy could consider what to do next, the plane had shot past the farm. In a minute they were over another group of buildings, then clusters of houses,

and then houses and other buildings packed tightly together. Sammy swooped down to get a better look.

The street had filled with hundreds of people. Some lined the sidewalks, waving and calling and cheering. Others marched down the middle of the street, followed by cars and pickup trucks, tractors, and fire trucks.

Sammy thought he saw someone familiar down below. "It looks like Hank…and Jimmy!" He maneuvered the plane for a better view, not realizing how low to the ground he had gotten. The *Spirit* was headed directly toward a large banner that was stretched across the street.

"Sammy!" Phoebe squealed. "Watch it!"

The *Spirit* flew right into the banner. The whining propeller ripped the fabric and a

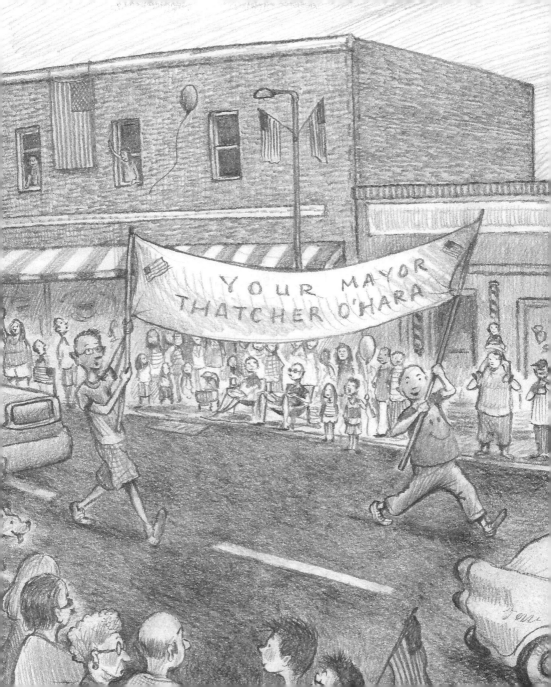

long piece got caught in the *Spirit's* landing gear, trailing behind the plane. Another fragment flattened across the windshield, blocking Sammy's view.

"I'll get it!" Phoebe leaned out the little window and tugged at the shredded banner.

The *Spirit* zoomed up and around crazily as Sammy tried to see where he was going. "Phoebe!" he yelled. "Be careful!"

She pulled the paper remnant away from the windshield and Sammy saw that they were heading directly toward a building.

"Whoooaa!" they shrieked together.

Sammy pulled at the controls and the *Spirit* zipped upwards. He yanked at them again and the plane spiraled back toward the ground.

On the street, faces looked up. "Hey!" someone called out. "What's that?"

Another banner appeared in front of them. "Up, Sammy! Up!" cried Phoebe.

He pulled on the controls one more time and the plane lifted, but not quite in time. The landing gear snagged the banner, and the *Spirit* pulled it through the air.

"Sammy!" Grace shouted. "Something's caught on the wheels!"

"We can't reach it!" squeaked Peewee.

The crowd shouted in amazement.

Sammy rocked the plane back and forth and dislodged the banner, which floated lazily into the waving arms of the spectators.

In control again, he angled the *Spirit* downward, right into the middle of Main Street. He was still going too fast. "I'm not sure how to stop it!" he cried out. "Prepare yourselves for a crash landing!"

But just then the *Spirit* slowed and began dropping gently. Phoebe looked out her window toward the rear of the plane. "It's Blackie!" she shouted.

Sammy looked back. Large black wings stuck out of the cargo door on each side of the plane. "Blackie is putting on his brakes!" Phoebe yelled out happily.

The plane slowed a bit and the shrill shrieking died down. The *Spirit* gently touched down on the yellow line, right down the middle of Main Street.

The *Spirit* had landed.

Hank and Jimmy pushed their way through the cheering crowd and darted to the airplane.

"Jimmy! Look!" Hank shouted. "It's the *Spirit of Sammy!*"

"Impossible!" Jimmy laughed. "I thought that plane was history!"

"I have to see if Sammy is all right," Hank panted, his feet racing under him.

"But how did that little squirt fly the plane back?" Jimmy asked.

"He is one smart mouse!" Hank shot back.

"This'll be the biggest thing to hit town, ever!" Jimmy shouted. "It's turning out just like I said. We'll be in all the papers!"

A crowd had surrounded the airplane.

"Stand back!" Jimmy warned. "The mouse needs room!"

A woman leaned out of her pickup truck. "Mouse?" she laughed. "Look!"

Blackie poked his head out of the *Spirit.* "That looks more like a crow to me!" the woman said. Blackie jumped from the cargo doorway down onto the pavement and cawed loudly.

"What the dickens?" Jimmy mumbled.

Just then a small reddish head peered out of the doorway.

"It's a newt!" said Hank. "A newt!"

The boys stared at Grace, then at each other.

A small, curiously sniffing nose appeared.

"And a shrew!" they both said in unison.

Hank looked inside the cockpit. A pink nose with white whiskers poked out of the window. "Sammy!" He scooped the mouse up and held him close. "I can't believe it. I never, ever thought I would see you again."

"And somebody else!" Jimmy exclaimed. "Look!"

Another set of twitching whiskers poked out the cockpit window.

Hank laughed. "Sammy found a friend! A whole set of friends!"

Jimmy leaped up onto the bed of the truck and faced the crowd. "This airplane," he declared, "the *Spirit of Sammy*, has just made a historic flight. In the footsteps of the great Charles Lindbergh, Sammy the mouse has gone where no mouse has gone before, traveling to distant horizons and to great heights." He looked at Hank, who was cradling Sammy and Phoebe under his chin. "He laughed in the face of fear. He challenged gravity itself. This is a great, great mouse."

"Hey, hold it right there, son." A man held up a camera and focused on Hank and the two mice. *Snap! Snap!* The sound of cameras flashing filled the air as everyone in the crowd cheered and clapped and laughed.

"Come on, Sammy," Hank murmured. "And your friends. Let's go home. Did you miss your shoe box?"

Jimmy gathered Peewee and Grace into his cap. "Here," he said, handing it to Hank. "You

take these guys. I'll grab the *Spirit.*" He gently maneuvered Blackie back into the airplane, then lifted it up onto his shoulder. "Let's go."

They walked down the street, past the last house in town, and headed across the fields to the farm.

CHAPTER 22

The summer days got shorter. The excitement of the historic flight of the *Spirit* eventually died down.

Photographers had come and gone. The reporters that had interviewed Hank and Jimmy day after day had long since stopped showing up on the front porch.

Sammy's old shoe box was gone. It had been replaced by a row of brand new cages, each filled with fresh sawdust, all donated by the local bank.

Phoebe gazed out the window. The leaves

of the large sugar maple in the yard outside Hank's bedroom were starting to turn yellow along their edges.

"I wonder how Grandfather is doing," she said "He must have stopped worrying about me by now."

"I wonder the same thing," Sammy sighed. "Osmund is so frail. And I wonder if Mustela has been leaving him alone now that he can't get his paws on the *Spirit*."

Their food dishes were heaped with delicacies. "Well, I wonder if good ol' Goggles is okay," Peewee said between nibbles. "Remember Mustela, swinging in that net? And the slippery roof?"

They all laughed.

Grace sat in a jar lid filled with water. "That was some airplane ride, wasn't it?" She swished her foot lazily through the water, staring at the ripples. "We were soooo high. A thing of beauty is a joy forever, that's what I always say."

Blackie grinned. "Highest I've ever been," he cawed. From where he perched on the top of the door to Hank's room he could see down into Sammy's cage. "The wind in my face... passing all the other birds. And the view was amazing. Bird's-eye!" He looked wistfully over at the *Spirit*, sitting on the floor.

"Thank goodness for you helping to stop the *Spirit*, Blackie," Sammy said. "Don't know what we'd have done without your brakes."

"Oh…thanks, Sammy. You're welcome," Blackie said, flushed with pride.

"What about me nibbling the rope, Sammy?" asked Peewee.

"You were amazing, Peewee," Sammy replied. "We'd still be on that old roof battling Mustela if it wasn't for you."

Peewee sighed with satisfaction and nibbled a dried cricket.

They sat quietly for a while, each lost in their own thoughts.

Finally Sammy broke the silence. "Are you guys thinking what I'm thinking?" he asked.

"I sure hope so," Blackie cawed.

"Me too," Peewee said.

"Me three!" added Grace.

Phoebe looked at Sammy and then spoke quietly. "Are you thinking that we should pull the *Spirit* out onto the porch roof, crank the propeller, and fly back to the Woods for a little visit?"

Sammy squealed. "That's exactly what I was thinking, Phoebe!"

"And I was thinking the same thing!" cawed Blackie.

"Me too!" Peewee squeaked.

"Me three!" giggled Grace.

"I figure we can use the same plan Goggles had," Sammy said. "With some rope we can pull the plane out the open window to the roof.

The main problem will be firing up the engine. Blackie, I think you're the only one of us who can do it. Think you can?"

"You bet!" Blackie replied.

"Can you see any rope that we could use?" Phoebe asked him.

Blackie had already scanned the room. "Maybe something just as good," he replied. Hank's bathrobe lay draped across the footboard. Blackie pulled on one end of the terrycloth belt.

"You are definitely the brains of this outfit, Blackie," said Phoebe.

In a matter of minutes the *Spirit* sat under the north window of Hank's bedroom.

"Everybody on board," Sammy directed. "Except Blackie—you be ready, and jump on board as fast as you can when the engine starts up, okay?"

"Everybody set?" Phoebe squeaked. "Peewee?"

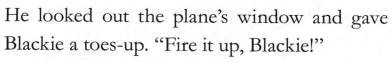

"Check!" he called.

"Grace?"

"Check!" she said.

Phoebe looked at Sammy. "Pilot ready?"

"Ready!" he shouted.

He looked out the plane's window and gave Blackie a toes-up. "Fire it up, Blackie!"

Blackie put his bill to one of the propeller blades and tapped it gently. "Here goes nothing!" He pushed down with all his might onto the blade. It spun in a short spurt.

Thwop!

He tried again.

Thwop!

And again. Each time the propeller engine

put out a little burst of energy, but then stopped quickly.

Thwop! Thwop!

"You can do it, Blackie!" Grace called out. "I know it!"

Blackie gasped for breath. With one final burst of energy he put all of his strength into pushing down on the propeller.

Thwop! THWOP! THWOP! THWOP! The engine roared to life and started its screaming, vibrating way down the porch roof.

"Now, Blackie! Now!" Sammy cried out.

But Blackie needed no encouragement. He hopped onto the *Spirit*, and Peewee and Grace grabbed him and pulled him on board.

The plane was getting closer to the edge.

"Hold on, everybody!" Phoebe shouted.

At the controls, Sammy gave the engine full

thrust and the *Spirit* came to life. The plane zoomed down the sloped roof, lifting off just as the gutter passed beneath her wheels, and took to the sky.

They came inches from hitting a telephone wire, and then veered over the top of an apple tree. They zipped over the small orchard and the barnyard, and then off over the back fields.

Sammy saw Hank and Jimmy down below in a field, chopping thistles. The two boys looked up, dumbfounded.

The engine hummed heartily as the *Spirit* soared high above the countryside. Sammy watched Hank and Jimmy get smaller and smaller, their white T-shirts becoming as tiny as clover blossoms, until they disappeared behind the folds of the hills.

Grace gave Blackie a pat. "Good job!" she yelled over the engine noise.

"Back in the air again!" Peewee squealed.

Phoebe smiled at Sammy. "Heading north, toward the Woods, right?" she asked.

"Right," Sammy answered.